# GRADUATION

## MOVING TO THE UNSEEN WORLD

# GRADUATION

# MOVING TO THE UNSEEN WORLD

TRIPLE T

ISBN: 979-8-9989700-8-5

This book mentions about cosmic events and cosmic phenomena that cannot be proven by the current scientific knowledges and technologies on Earth, therefore, it's a science fiction book. Take whatever you can resonate with and use it for your soul development purposes and leave behind whatever you cannot resonate with. For the evolution of the souls, it's like hatching an egg, the force must be cracked from inside out not from outside in.

To all cosmic entities on Earth and in the Known Universe

# Table of Contents

General Knowledge about Earth and Our Cosmos ............. 3

Seven Dimensions in the Universal Verse ....................... 27

Cosmic Soul Lessons from First Dimension to Seventh Dimension ..................................................................... 33

Intelligent Lifeforms in the Known Universe ................... 38

Origins of the Third Density Entities on Earth ............... 49

The Cosmic workers.......................................................... 64

The Cosmic Libraries ........................................................ 96

Extraterrestrials/Alien encounters ................................. 103

Third Density Entity Lifecycle on Earth ........................ 109

The Cosmic Creator School ............................................ 116

Volunteer Deities from the Godverse............................. 144

The Soul Evolutionary Processes in the Known Universe ........................................................................................ 160

Origins of the Known Universe ...................................... 189

The Merging.................................................................... 195

Summary and Final Thoughts ......................................... 205

About the Author............................................................. 218

Table of Large Numbers ................................................. 221

Notes from Triple T to the Third Density Entities that Are Worth Reading ................................................................ 223

# Chapter 1

# General Knowledge about Earth and Our Cosmos

The Known Universe is reported to be around 13.8 billion earth years by scientists on Earth based on the Big Bang theory. The truth is that, the Known Universe is much, much older than that. With the current technologies on Earth, it's impossible for any scientists to measure the actual age of the Known Universe. Scientists on Earth can only measure the age of the celestial objects that are closer to Earth in the Observable Universe at this current spacetime. Earth is located in the newly formed part of the Observable Universe. The Observable Universe is located in the newly formed part of the Known Universe. Therefore, using the age of the celestial objects in the Observable Universe to assume the age of the Known Universe is not accurate. The Known Universe has existed not only for a trillion earth years, but has already existed for about 300 trillion earth years. The age of planet Earth is much younger than the age of the Known Universe. It's a young planet located in a young and newly formed galaxy in the Known Universe.

Earth is located in a small star system called the Solar System. The Solar System is located in a spiral galaxy called the Milky Way galaxy. The Milky Way galaxy contains about a trillion star systems like the Solar System at this current spacetime. This number is constantly changing because the star systems within the Milky Way galaxy are constantly changing, evolving, and merging. The Milky Way galaxy is located in the Observable Universe. The Observable Universe is a spherical region of the Known Universe that contains all matter that can be observed from Earth. The Observable Universe contains trillions of galaxies like the Milky Way galaxy at this current spacetime. Each galaxy has hundred billion to hundred trillion star systems. The Observable Universe is only a tiny part of the Known Universe. With the limitations of technologies on Earth, scientists at this current spacetime only can observe the Known Universe with the distance of 46.5 billion light years in radius, which is about 93 billion light years across. Any galaxies or celestial objects beyond the 46.5 billion light years radius are invisible, unseeable and undetectable by the current technologies on Earth. The size of the Observable Universe will expend as technologies on Earth become more and more advanced which can observe and detect celestial objects further beyond the current Observable Universe. The size of the Observable Universe is only about 1/several hundred trillion googols the size of the Known Universe. The Known Universe is located in a larger cosmological hierarchy where different laws of physics apply called the Multiverse. Even though the size of the Known Universe is about several hundred trillion googol times larger than the size of the Observable Universe, the Known Universe only constitutes just a tiny or even infinitesimal subset of the Multiverse where the Known Universe is located. There are countless Multiverses. Each Multiverse consists of trillion googols to decillion googol Universes like the Known Universe. This number is constantly changing because the Universes within each Multiverse are constantly evolving, changing, and merging. (Googol is a number that has 100 zeros behind it. There's a scientific notation of table of large number at the end of this book for easy reference). The Multiverses are invisible and undetectable by any kinds of technologies on Earth.

As ginormous as the size of each Multiverse is, it only constitutes a tiny part of another larger cosmological hierarchy where different laws of physics apply called the Megaverse. There are countless Megaverses. Each Megaverse consists of hundred centillion Multiverses. This number is constantly changing because the Multiverses within each Megaverse are constantly evolving, changing, and merging. Everything in the Megaverse is unmeasurable, unimaginable and undetectable by any kinds of technologies on Earth. No matter how advance technologies on Earth will be in the future, it will never be able to detect anything beyond the Known Universe. No matter how ginormous and humongous the Megaverse is, it only constitutes a tiny part of another larger cosmological hierarchy called the Gigaverse. There are countless Gigaverses. Each Gigaverse consists of billion centillions to trillion centillion Megaverses. This number is constantly changing because the Megaverses within each Gigaverse are constantly evolving, changing, and merging. Everything in the Gigaverse is unimaginable and completely beyond the comprehension of any third density entities on Earth. Another larger cosmological hierarchy beyond the Gigaverse is the Archverse. There are countless Archverses. Each Archverse comprises of trillion centillions to septillion centillion Gigaverses. This number is constantly changing because the Gigaverses within each Archverse are constantly evolving, changing, and merging. Like the Gigaverse, everything in the Archverse is completely beyond the comprehension of any third density entities on Earth.

The highest cosmological hierarchy where planet Earth is located in the lower realm of the Cosmos is the Goongverse. The Goongverse consists of countless Archverses. It's a complete totality of all verses as well as visible and invisible matter, space, and time in the Goongverse in the lower realm. Beyond the Goongverse is the divine realm where the Creatorverse, the Godverse, and the Infinite Creatorverse are located. The Creatorverse is home to any creators or any entities who have the cosmic powers as high as the creator level. There are two verses in the Creatorverse at this current spacetime. These two verses only constitute a tiny part of the Creatorverse. These two verses orbit around the Goongverse. Each of these two verses only has one entity residing in it. One verse belongs to the Creator of the Goongverse and the other verse belongs to the Creator of the Goongverse's opponent which is the Anti Creator. These two entities are constantly keeping an eye on the development processes of the entities in the Goongverse. Each entity has different purposes. One is constantly creating and infusing positive energy into the Goongverse while the other one is constantly trying to demolish and infuse negative energy into the Goongverse. Beyond the Creatorverse is the Godverse. The Godverse is home to the Gods and Deities. Beyond the Godverse is the Infinite Godverse. This is the highest impossible, the unthinkable reality in our vast cosmos. It includes everything that exists in our cosmos like the Goongverse, the Creatorverse, the Godverse, countless other Verses, the Voids, the Beyond, and all cosmic matter, space, and time, etc. The Infinite Godverse is home to only one entity. That entity is the Infinite Creator of our Cosmos. There are many other Cosmoses in the Grand Cosmos that are completely beyond the comprehension of any entities from our Cosmos. Not even the Infinite Creator of our Cosmos has complete access to the knowledges of other Cosmoses at this current spacetime.

Our Cosmos is so vast and so massive that it's completely unmeasurable by any kind of technologies on Earth or on any other planets in the Goongverse. Earth is like a tiny piece of sand in all the beaches on Earth combined in the Known Universe. The Known Universe is like a tiny piece of sand in all the beaches on Earth combined in the Multiverse where the Known Universe is located. The Multiverse is like a tiny piece of sand in all the beaches on Earth combined in the Megaverse where the Multiverse is located. The Megaverse is like a tiny piece of sand in all the beaches on Earth combined in the Gigaverse where the Megaverse is located. The Gigaverse is like a tiny piece of sand in all the beaches on Earth combined in the Archverse where the Gigaverse is located. The Archverse is like a tiny piece of sand in all the beaches in the Known Universe and all the beaches in other Universes in the entire universal verse combined in the Goongverse. Just imagine if all planets in every verse in the Goongversal hierarchy have beaches like Earth, then the Goongverse is like a tiny piece of sand in all the beaches in all the Universes, all the Multiverses, all the Megaverses, all the Gigaverses, all the Archverses, and the whole Goongverse combined in our Cosmos.

Despite the fact that there are many different verses operate with different laws of physics in the Goongverse, the soul development processes of intelligent lifeforms and non-intelligent lifeforms are the same if they reside in the same verse or the same dimension throughout the Goongverse. The soul development processes of any lifeforms don't depend on which location they are residing in, it depends on which verse or which dimension they are residing in and the vibrational frequency of each entity in different cosmic dimensions. For example, there are planets in the Known Universe where Earth is located can support the third dimensional lifeforms, there also planets in other Universes besides the Known Universe can support the third dimensional lifeforms. The physical appearances of the third dimensional lifeforms might look different on/in different planets or different Universes, however, the soul development processes of all the third dimensional lifeforms would be the same since they all residing in the same dimension and the same verse within the Goongverse.

There are twenty-seven dimensions in the Goongverse. In each dimension, there are seven sub-dimensions within it. In each sub-dimension, there are seven sub-sub-dimensions within it. For example, in the first dimension there are sub-dimensions such as 1.1, 1.2...and 1.7. In the 1.1 sub-dimension, there are sub-sub-dimension such as: 1.1.1, 1.1.2 ...and 1.1.7. In the second dimension, there are sub-dimensions such as 2.1, 2.2...and 2.7. In the 2.1 sub-dimension, there are sub-sub-dimension such as 2.1.1, 2.1.2... and 2.1.7, so on and so on. In each dimension or sub-dimension, there are great numbers of lifeforms residing in it. Lifeforms in different dimensions or different sub-dimensions vibrate in different frequencies and have different cosmic lessons to learn. Lifeforms in higher dimensions vibrate in higher vibrational frequencies and lifeforms in lower dimensions vibrate in lower vibrational frequencies.

In the universal verse, each Universe can support lifeforms from the first dimension up to the seventh dimension. This means that entities who are residing in any Universes in the universal verse can either be the first density

9

entities, the second density entities, the third density entities, the fourth density entities, the fifth density entities, the sixth density entities or the seventh density entities. Humans on Earth are the third density entities in the Known Universe. They are currently in the process of learning their third dimensional cosmic lessons in order to graduate and move up to the fourth dimension where they will learn their next level of cosmic lessons. When they have learned all of the seven dimensional cosmic lessons in the Known Universe, they would be able to exit the Known Universe and move up to the Multiverse where the Known Universe is located. This process could take up billions of earth years. For slow learning entities, this process could even take up trillions of earth years or even longer than that.

In the multiversal verse, each Multiverse can support lifeforms from the eighth dimension up to the eleventh dimension. This means that entities who are residing in any Multiverses in the multiversal verse can either be the eighth density entities, the ninth density entities, the tenth density entities or the eleventh density entities. When the multiversal entities have learned all of their cosmic lessons from the eighth dimension up to the eleventh dimension, they would be able to graduate and exit the Multiverse. They would move up to the Megaverse where their host Multiverse is located to learn their next level of cosmic lessons.

In the megaversal verse, each Megaverse can support lifeforms from the twelfth dimension up to the fifteenth dimension. This means that entities who are residing in any Megaverses in the megaversal verse can either be the twelfth density entities, the thirteenth density entities, the fourteenth density entities or the fifteenth density entities. When all the cosmic lessons in the megaversal verse have been learned, the megaversal entities can graduate and exit their host Megaverse. They will move up to the Gigaverse where their host Megaverse is located to learn their next level of cosmic lessons. Any cosmic lessons in the megaversal verse and in the verses beyond the megaversal verse in the goongversal hierarchy are completely beyond the comprehension of any third density entities in the universal verse.

In the gigaversal verse, each Gigaverse can support lifeforms from the sixteenth dimension up to the nineteenth dimension. This means that entities who are residing in any Gigaverses in the gigaversal verse can either be the sixteenth density entities, the seventeenth density entities, the eighteenth density entities or the nineteenth density entities. When all the cosmic lessons in the gigaversal verse have been learned, the gigaversal entities can graduate and exit their host Gigaverse. They will move up to the Archverse where their host Gigaverse is located to learn their next level of cosmic lessons.

In the archversal verse, each Archverse can support lifeforms from the twentieth dimension up to the twenty-third dimension. This means that entities who are residing in any Archverses in the archversal verse can either be the twentieth density entities, the twenty-first density entities, the twenty-second density entities or the twenty-third density entities. When the archversal entities have learned all of their cosmic lessons in their host Archverse, they can graduate and exit their host Archverse. They will move up to the Goongverse to learn their final cosmic lessons to prepare themselves to graduate and exit the Goongverse.

The Goongverse can support lifeforms from the twenty-fourth dimension up to the twenty-seventh dimension. This means that entities who are residing in the highest hierarchy of the Goongverse can either be the twenty-fourth density entities, the twenty-fifth density entities, the twenty-sixth density entities or the twenty-seventh density entities. When all the cosmic lessons in the Goongverse have been learned. The goongversal entities would completely become godlike and would be able to graduate and exit the Goongverse. They will move up to the Creatorverse to become the true cosmic creators. Exiting from the Goongverse to the Creatorverse is the most difficult thing to do for any entities in the Goongverse.

Dimensions in the Creatorverse, the Godverse, and the Infinite Godverse are incomprehensible by any entities in the Goongverse. Only those entities who have learned all of the twenty-seven dimensional cosmic lessons in the Goongverse and ready to exit the Goongverse would be able to perceive and comprehend.

Even though there are so many dimensions in the Goongverse and the Creator of the Goongverse, the Deities, the Gods, and the Infinite Creator seem so far for the lower density entities to reach, there are actually entities that are godlike in every verse in the goongversal hierarchy. The godlike entities that the third density entities on Earth come to contact with are the little Gods, not the Creator from the Creatorverse or the Gods from the Godverse or the Infinite Creator from the Infinite Godverse. The little Gods that the third density entities on Earth or on any other third dimensional planets in the Known Universe come to contact with are the higher density entities in the Known Universe. They are either the fourth density entities, the fifth density entities, the sixth density entities or the seventh density entities in the Known Universe. Since the higher density entities are far more powerful and far more capable of doing unimaginable things that the third density entities cannot do, the third density entities on Earth or on any other third dimensional planets mistakenly think of them as the Creator of the Goongverse, or the Gods, or the Infinite Creator. The knowledge about the Creator of the Goongverse, the Gods, or the Infinite Creator is very limited to the third density entities on Earth and the third density entities on any other third dimensional planets. Whatever they thought they know about the Creator of the Goongverse, the Gods, or the Infinite Creator, or the ways they describe them usually are the descriptions of the higher density entities in the Known Universe. For the third density entities in other Universes, they also think of the higher density entities within their host

Universe as Gods, as the Creator of the Goongverse or as the Infinite Creator.

There are many teachings about the soul evolutionary processes to the third density entities on Earth and to the third density entities on other third dimensional planets in the Known Universe and other Universes, but none of the teachings have gone beyond the universal verse. They all think that the highest dimension in their host Universe in the universal verse is the highest dimension in the Cosmos where the Infinite Creator would reside. This is because the cosmic workers who volunteered to come to Earth or volunteered to go to other planets to assist the third density entities with their third dimensional cosmic lessons are mainly come from the fourth, the fifth, and the sixth dimensions within their host Universe, they don't have access to any other Universes besides their host Universe or have access to any other higher verses beyond the universal verse like the Multiverse, the Megaverse or the Gigaverse, etc.

The Creator of the Goongverse is constantly infusing positive energy into the Goongverse while his opponent, the Anti Creator, is constantly infusing negative energy into the Goongverse, therefore, in every dimension and every verse in the Goongverse, living entities can either polarize positively or negatively. For the positive polarized entities, not only they can graduate from one dimension and move up to the next dimension within the same verse but they can also graduate from one verse and move up to another verse when they have learned all of their cosmic lessons in that particular dimension or particular verse. For the negative polarized entities, they can only move from one dimension to the next dimension within the same verse. They cannot move from one verse to another verse. For them to be able to exit one verse and move up to the next verse, they would have to reset and relearn their cosmic lessons from the dimension where they first started to polarize negatively and they must turn to polarize positively. If they still polarize negatively, they would have to reset and relearn their cosmic lessons from the dimension where they first started to polarize negatively over again. There are negative polarized entities in every verse in the Goongverse, but this doesn't mean that the negative polarized entities in the higher verses in the goongversal hierarchy are actually the negative polarized entities from the lower verses who graduated and moved up to. In every verse in the Goongverse, there are entities who would turn to polarize negatively because of the effects of the negative energy that the Anti Creator constantly infusing into different verses within the Goongverse.

Graduating or exiting from one verse to the next verse is impossible for any negative polarized entities. The Creator of the Goongverse does not allow that and the Anti Creator has never been able to find a way to go around it. The highest dimension the negative polarized entities in each verse can move up to is one dimension below the highest dimension in their host verse. For example, in the universal verse, the highest dimension the negative entities can move up to is the sixth dimension. They cannot move up to the highest dimension in the universal verse which is the seventh dimension. Once they move up to the highest sub-dimension of the sixth dimension, which is the 6.7 sub-dimension, they have to reset and relearn their cosmic lessons from the beginning or from whichever dimension in the universal verse where they started to polarize negatively. In the multiversal verse, the negative polarized entities cannot move all the way up to the eleventh dimension, which is the highest dimension in the multiversal verse. The highest dimension the negative polarized entities can move up to in the multiversal verse is the tenth dimension. When they move up to the highest sub-dimension of the tenth dimension, which is the 10.7 sub-dimension, they would be reset so they can relearn their cosmic lessons from the beginning or from whichever dimension in the multiversal verse where they first started to polarize negatively.

Since the beginning of the Goongverse up until this current spacetime, no negative polarized entities have ever been able to exit one verse and move up to the next verse. They can only move up to the dimension below the highest dimension in their host verse. They have to reset and restart learning their cosmic lessons over and over again until they turn to polarize positively and make their way up to the highest dimension in their host verse, by then, they can exit their host verse and move up to the next verse. Negative polarized entities have no idea about the resetting; they keep thinking that they can make their ways up to the highest dimension in the Goongverse or the highest dimension in the Cosmos. Some negative polarized entities don't even realize that they are actually polarizing negatively.

Planets or stars or galaxies that have more positive polarized entities residing in/on usually polarize positively throughout the Goongverse. Planets or stars or galaxies that have more negative polarized entities residing in/on usually polarize negatively throughout the Goongverse.

Each planet, star, or galaxy itself is a living entity in the Goongverse. Planets in lower dimensions can support lifeforms in lower dimensions or lower density entities. Planets in higher dimensions can support lifeforms in higher dimensions or higher density entities. The vibrational frequencies of intelligent lifeforms have great impact on the vibrational frequencies of the planet which they are residing in/on. Stars or dwarf stars usually support higher dimensional lifeforms since they have higher vibrational frequencies as compare to planets or celestial objects that orbiting around them.

For the third density entities on Earth at this current spacetime, the main thing they need to do is to focus on learning their third dimensional cosmic lessons so they can graduate and move up to the fourth dimension. The final goal of all the universal entities is to learn all of the seven dimensional cosmic lessons so they can exit their host

Universe and move up to the Multiverse where their host Universe is located to learn their next level of cosmic lessons. Exiting from the universal verse and move up to the multiversal verse is the third most difficult thing to do for any entities. The most difficult thing for any entities to do is exiting the twenty seventh dimension of the Goongverse and move up to the Creatorverse. The second most difficult thing for any entities to do is graduating from the third dimension and move up to the fourth dimension in the universal verse.

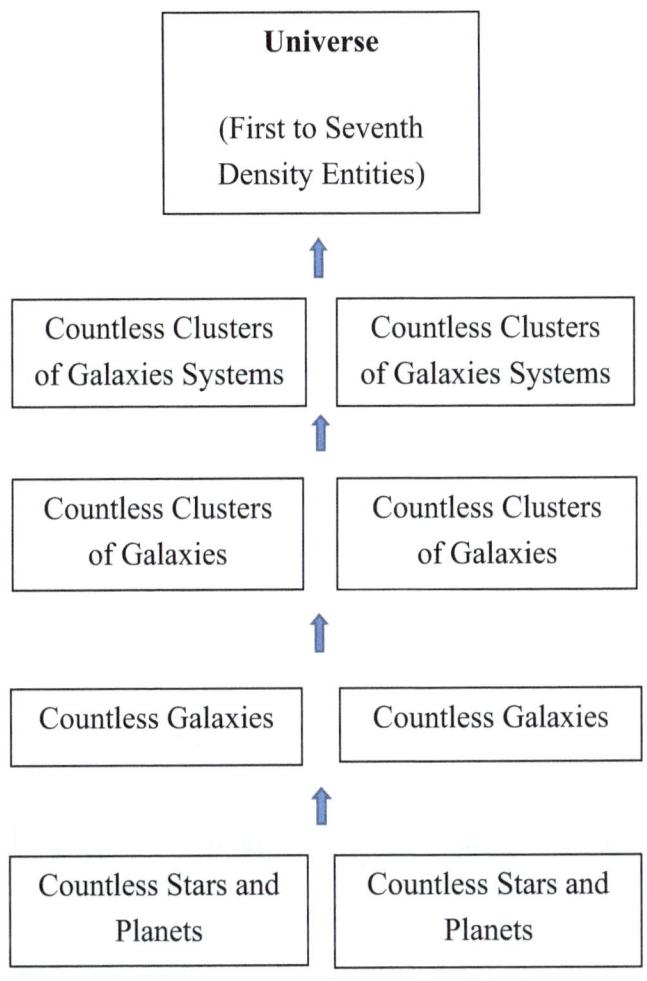

Each individual Universe comprises of countless clusters of galaxies systems, countless clusters of galaxies, countless galaxies, and countless stars and planets.

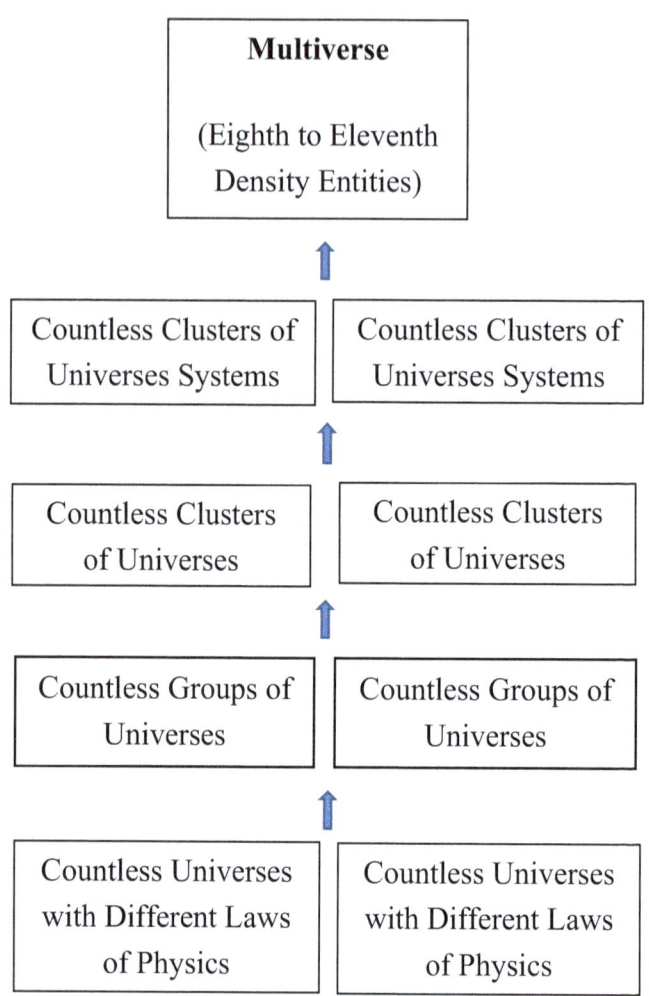

Each individual Multiverse comprises of countless clusters of universes systems, countless clusters of universes, countless groups of universes, and countless Universes which operate with different laws of physics.

| **Megaverse** |
|:---:|
| (Twelfth to Fifteenth Density Entities) |

| Countless Clusters of Multiverses Systems | Countless Clusters of Multiverses Systems |
|:---:|:---:|

| Countless Clusters of Multiverses | Countless Clusters of Multiverses |
|:---:|:---:|

| Countless Multiverses with Different Laws of Physics | Countless Multiverses with Different Laws of Physics |
|:---:|:---:|

Each Megaverse comprises of countless clusters of multiverses systems, countless clusters of multiverses, and countless Multiverses which operate with different laws of physics.

**Gigaverse**

(Sixteenth to Nineteenth
Density Entities)

| Countless Clusters of Megaverses Systems | Countless Clusters of Megaverses Systems |
|---|---|

| Countless Clusters of Megaverses | Countless Clusters of Megaverses |
|---|---|

| Countless Megaverses with Different Laws of Physics | Countless Megaverses with Different Laws of Physics |
|---|---|

Each Gigaverse comprises of countless clusters of megaverses systems, countless clusters of megaverses, and countless Megaverses which operate with different laws of physics.

```
┌─────────────────────────────────┐
│           Archverse             │
│                                 │
│    (Twentieth to Twenty-Third   │
│        Density Entities)        │
└─────────────────────────────────┘
                ⬆
┌──────────────────┐ ┌──────────────────┐
│ Countless Clusters of │ │ Countless Clusters of │
│ Gigaverses Systems    │ │ Gigaverses Systems    │
└──────────────────┘ └──────────────────┘
                ⬆
┌──────────────────┐ ┌──────────────────┐
│ Countless Clusters of │ │ Countless Clusters of │
│ Gigaverses            │ │ Gigaverses            │
└──────────────────┘ └──────────────────┘
                ⬆
┌──────────────────┐ ┌──────────────────┐
│ Countless Gigaverses  │ │ Countless Gigaverses  │
│ with Different Laws   │ │ with Different Laws   │
│ of Physics            │ │ of Physics            │
└──────────────────┘ └──────────────────┘
```

Each Archverse comprises of countless clusters of gigaverses systems, countless clusters of gigaverses, and countless Gigaverses which operate with different laws of physics.

| Goongverse |
|:---:|
| (Twenty-Fourth to Twenty-Seventh Density Entities) |

⬆

| Countless Clusters of Archverses Systems | Countless Clusters of Archverses Systems |
|:---:|:---:|

⬆

| Countless Clusters of Archverses | Countless Clusters of Archverses |
|:---:|:---:|

⬆

| Countless Archverses with Different Laws of Physics | Countless Archverses with Different Laws of Physics |
|:---:|:---:|

The Goongverse comprises of countless clusters of archverses systems, countless clusters of archverses, and countless Archverses which operate with different laws of physics.

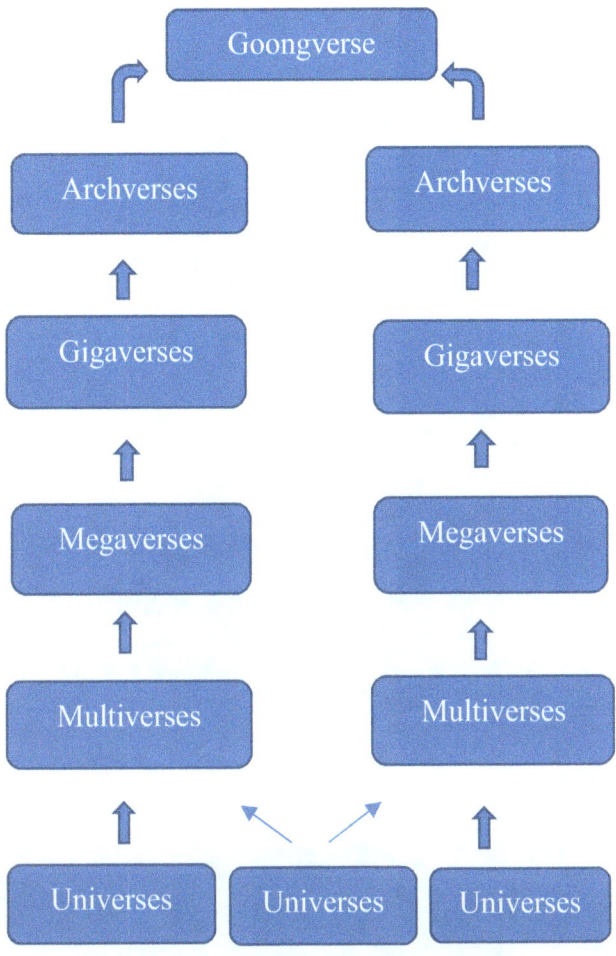

Within the Goongverse, there are countless Archverses. Within each Archverse, there are countless Gigaverses. Within each Gigaverse, there are countless Megaverses. Within each Megaverse, there are countless Multiverses. Within each Multiverse, there are countless Universes. Within each Universe, there are countless galaxies and clusters of galaxies.

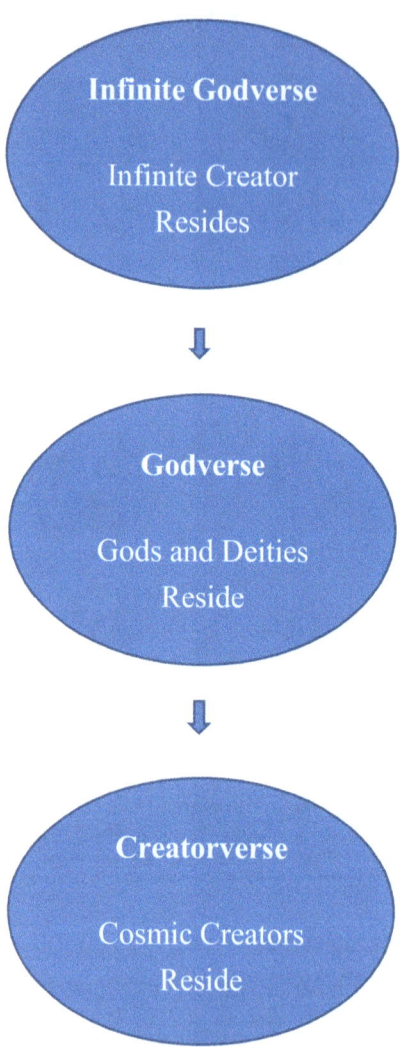

The three highest verses in the divine realm in our Cosmos

# Chapter 2

# Seven Dimensions in the Universal Verse

Each individual Universe in the universal verse can support lifeforms from the first dimension up to the seventh dimension. The first three dimensions in the universal verse are the physical plane of the Goongverse. In order to exist and experience life in the physical plane, all entities must take some kind of physical forms. Lower cosmic entities use the physical forms as the operating vehicles for them to learn their cosmic lessons in the lower dimensions in the physical plane. From the fourth dimension up to the seventh dimension are the lower astral plane of the Goongverse. The fourth dimension is the lowest dimension in the astral plane. Starting from the fourth dimension and up, living entities are not necessarily need to take any kinds of physical forms in order to exist. They have their astral forms which normally cannot be seen by any third density entities. Entities from the higher dimensions can see entities from the lower dimensions, but entities from the lower dimensions cannot see entities from the higher dimensions unless the entities from the higher dimensions want to show themselves to the entities in the lower dimensions or certain entities in the lower dimensions have very high vibrational frequencies can see the entities from the higher dimensions.

First dimensional lifeforms in the Known Universe are elements such as rocks, dirt, or minerals, etc. Second dimensional lifeforms in the Known Universe are living things that have low vibrational frequencies such as animals, plants, or trees... Trees are very unique entities. Trees mainly vibrate in the vibrational frequencies of the second density entities, but some trees can raise up its vibrational frequencies and vibrate in the vibrational frequencies of the third density entities. Some trees could even reach up to the vibrational frequencies of the fourth density entities. Third dimensional lifeforms in the Known Universe are the entities that vibrate in the same frequencies as humans on Earth at this current spacetime. Humans on Earth are mainly vibrating in the frequencies of the third density entities, but for some entities, especially those who are already awakened or fully enlightened could vibrate in the frequencies of the fourth density entities or could even reach up to the vibrational frequencies of the fifth density entities at this current spacetime. Entities in the third dimension can only see entities from the first dimension up to the third dimension. Entities from the fourth dimension or higher are generally invisible to them. Only certain entities in the third dimension with high vibrational frequencies can tap into the frequencies of the fourth dimension or higher and be able to see entities from the fourth dimension or higher. To the third density entities, the fourth density entities or higher density entities would appear godlike to them. The highest dimension in the universal verse is the seventh dimension. The seventh dimension is like the Godverse to the third density entities on Earth or on any other third dimensional planets. At this current spacetime, none of the third density entities on Earth have any knowledge of any Universes besides the Known Universe or any verses that exist beyond the universal verse. There are some teachings on Earth which added some dimensions beyond the seventh dimension in the Known Universe, but they are actually talking about different sub-dimensions of the seventh dimension in the Known Universe, not any dimensions beyond the Known Universe or beyond the universal verse.

There are little creators in every dimension and every verse in the Goongverse. All cosmic entities in the Goongverse have creator instinct within them. Lower density entities can create, build, or manage things or celestial objects that are far less complex and in much smaller scale. Higher density entities can create, build, and manage things or celestial objects that are far more complex and in much larger scale. In the universal verse, the second density entities are capable of building shelters for themselves. The third density entities are capable of building shelters, roads, airplanes, spaceships and even satellites or satellite planets that orbiting around their host planet. The fourth density entities can build, create and manage a planet and its moons like the Earth and its moon or Jupiter and its moons. The fourth density entities are the planetary creators.

The fifth density entities can build, create, and manage a star system like the Solar System or the Alpha Centauri System. They are the star system creators. The sixth density entities can build, create, and manage a galaxy and its dwarf galaxies like the Milky Way galaxy or the Andromeda Galaxy. They are the galactic creators. The seventh density entities can create, arrange and manage cluster of galaxies within their host Universe. They are the entities that keeping their host Universe functioning properly without collapsing. They are the highest creators in their host Universe. The seventh density entities are also the entities that are in charge of creating, protecting, managing, and keeping peace between intelligent lifeforms within their host Universe in the universal verse.

There is one highest council within each individual Universe, which is the Universal Council. Members of the Universal Council are mainly the seventh density entities. The Universal Council is in charge of overseeing the soul evolutionary processes of all the entities from the first dimension up to the seventh dimension within their host Universe. They can change, recreate or redesign the physical bodies, the astral bodies, or the lifecycles of any entities or planetary entities below the seventh dimension. Below the Universal Council is the Galactic Council. The Galactic Council comprises of mainly the sixth density entities and some seventh density entities. Members of the Galactic Council are mainly in charge of carrying out the missions that assigned by the Universal Council.

Lifespan of the third density entities in the universal verse can be ranging between 100 to 1000 earth years. Lifespan of the third density entities on Earth at this current spacetime is about 100 earth years while lifespan of the third density entities on other planets in the Known Universe or in other Universes can reach up to 1000 earth years. Lifespan of the fourth density entities on average is about 300 thousand to 500 thousand earth years. Lifespan of the fifth density entities on average is about 5 million to 10 million earth years. Lifespan of the sixth density entities can be varied the most. It can be ranging between 20 million earth years to about 500 million earth years depending on which paths they choose to learn their sixth dimensional cosmic lessons and which type of stars they are residing in/on. (This will be discussed in later chapter of this book). Lifespan of the seventh density entities on average is about 1 billion to 1.2 billion earth years. Because of the distortion of spacetime in different dimensions, the measurements above are only about 90 to 95% accurate.

The most difficult graduation in the universal verse is the graduation from the third dimension to the fourth dimension which is the graduation from the physical plane to the lower astral plane. It's the second most difficult graduation in the entire Goongverse right after the graduation from the Goongverse to the Creatorverse. This is the graduation that the third density entities on Earth are currently going through. Seventh dimension is the highest dimension in the universal verse. When an entity reaches to the seventh dimension, he or she can choose to remain there for a long time to help with the management of their host Universe without trying to exit their host Universe immediately even though he or she already learned all of the seventh dimensional cosmic lessons. The seventh density entities are the most powerful entities in the universal verse. For the lower density entities, the seventh density entities are like Gods or the Creator of the Goongverse, or the Infinite Creator to them. Seventh dimension is the dimension that any entities in the lower dimensions in the universal verse would strive for.

For the seventh density entities who have learned all of their cosmic lessons in the lower sub-dimensions of the seventh dimension and are in the highest sub-dimension of the seventh dimension learning their final cosmic lessons in the universal verse, they no longer emitting light that can be seen or detected by any technologies on Earth at this current spacetime. Maybe in the future, the third density entities on Earth would be able to develop advanced technologies that can detect the type of light that the seventh density entities from the highest sub-dimension of the seventh dimension emitting out. A few third density entities from other third dimensional planets that have extreme advanced technologies can detect it at this current spacetime. These seventh density entities usually reside in places that scientists on Earth called black holes or black dwarf stars in the universal verse.

# Chapter 3

# Cosmic Soul Lessons from First Dimension to Seventh Dimension

First dimension is the lowest dimension in the universal verse. Living entities in the first dimension have very low vibrational frequencies. First dimension is the dimension of beingness or the very beginning of consciousness. Consciousness is in its development stage or in its waking up stage. When the first density entities have the experience close to self-awareness, they starting to have desire to generate growth. As they want to generate growth, the very beginning of starting to think for each individual arises, they become more independent in the desire for self exploration. Once the desire for growth and self exploration started to arise, they can move up to the second dimension to learn their next level of cosmic lessons.

Second dimension is the dimension of growing towards independence and self-awareness. When the second density entities generate enough of a vibration of self-awareness, they can move up to the third dimension to learn their next level of cosmic lessons.

Third dimension is the dimension of separation and self-consciousness. In the third dimension, each entity sees himself or herself as a separate entity in comparison to other entities. In order for the second density entities to graduate and move up to the third dimension, they must develop enough self-awareness and learn to separate themselves from their packs or groups as an individual entity.

Fourth dimension is the dimension of love and compassion. In order to graduate and move up to the fourth dimension, the third density entities must learn the cosmic lessons of love and compassion. They must learn how to love others like how they would love themselves and have unconditional love for everyone around them or whoever they come into contact with. This path is the path for positive polarized entities. Starting from the third dimension, the negative energy from the Anti Creator started to affect each individual entity clearly. Each entity would start to polarize either positively or negatively starting from the third dimension. The first and second density entities have little or no effect from the negative energy from the Anti Creator since they still mainly behave base on their survival instincts. For the third negative polarized density entities to graduate and move up to the fourth dimension as negative entities, they must devote 98% of their time loving themselves. They must also generate enough negative energy and create enough pain and chaos in each incarnation in order for them to move up to the fourth dimension as negative entities. Graduation for the positive polarized entities is easier than the graduation for the negative polarized entities. In order to graduate and move up to the fourth dimension as positive entities, the third positive polarized density entities only need to provide 51% of their services to serve others, to love others, and to care for others while for graduation and move up to the fourth dimension as negative polarized entities, the third negative polarized density entities need to perform above 98% of their services to serve themselves. They must also create enough negative energy and pain in order to qualify. If they ever reach up to the highest sub-dimension of the sixth dimension one day, they would have to reset and restart learning their cosmic lessons from the third dimension again. They have to repeat this process until they turn to polarize positively and consistently polarizing positively throughout all seven dimensions in the universal verse, by then they can graduate and exit their host Universe and move up to the Multiverse where their host Universe is located. If they turn to polarize negatively again in the fourth or the fifth dimension, they would have to restart learning their cosmic lessons again in the fourth or the fifth dimension.

Fifth dimension is the dimension of wisdom. In order to graduate and move up to the fifth dimension, the fourth density entities must gain enough wisdom and knowledge about their host Universe and know the existence of different dimensions in their host Universe. They must understand how their Universe works and how things operate in different dimensions within their host Universe. There is so much knowledge about each individual Universe and the higher dimensions that the third density entities on Earth and the third density entities on any other third dimensional planets are not capable of knowing or understanding due to the limitations of their third dimensional functional brains. So much knowledges about each individual Universe that cannot be accessed by the third density entities on Earth or the third density entities on any other third dimensional planets. The third density entities will have the ability to access to some of these knowledges and capable of understanding once they have graduated and moved up to the fourth dimension.

Sixth dimension is the dimension of balancing between love and wisdom. In order to graduate and move up to the sixth dimension, the fifth density entities must learn how to balance between love and wisdom throughout their whole incarnation. Sixth dimension is the dimension where the sixth negative polarized density entities in the highest sub-dimension of the sixth dimension have to reset in order for them to relearn their cosmic lessons from the dimension where they first started to polarize negatively.

Seventh dimension is the dimension of understanding and unity. It's the highest dimension in the universal verse. In order to graduate and move up to the seventh dimension, the sixth density entities must understand how everything works throughout their host Universe. They must understand how everything works in the soul evolutionary processes in different dimensions. Only the sixth positive polarized density entities who have learned all of their sixth dimensional cosmic lessons can graduate and move up to the seventh dimension. The sixth negative polarized density entities cannot graduate and move up to the seventh dimension. They have to reset and relearn their cosmic lessons again from the dimension where they first started to polarize negatively.

Eighth dimension is the lowest dimension in the multiversal verse. In order for the seventh density entities to graduate from their host Universe and move up to the Multiverse where their host Universe is located, they must learn how things work in the lowest dimension in the Multiverse where they are about to graduate and move up to. They must learn all the necessary skills in order to build, create, and manage a Universe with matter, particle and energy that they can control and have access to. The eighth density entities must know how to keep the orbit of each individual Universe within the Multiverse from colliding with one another. The seventh density entities who wish to stay longer in the seventh dimension to help with the soul development processes of the lower density entities in their host Universe would mainly focus their time in creating, managing, aiding, and keeping harmony between intelligent lifeforms within their host Universe.

# Chapter 4

# Intelligent Lifeforms in the Known Universe

The universal verse is full of intelligent lifeforms. Octillion centillions to nonillion centillion intelligent lifeforms are currently residing in the Known Universe. Scientists on Earth can't see or detect them because majority of them living in different dimensions and vibrating in different frequencies. Technologies on Earth are not advanced enough in order to detect any living lifeforms beyond the third dimensional lifeforms in the physical plane. The planets that supporting the third dimensional lifeforms in the Known Universe at this current spacetime are kind of far for technologies on Earth to reach. Scientists on Earth can send spaceships to different planets to look for signs of intelligent lifeforms, but if the planet they are exploring not supporting the second or the third dimensional lifeforms, that planet would appear empty as if there's nothing living on/in it. But there are actually plentiful of higher dimensional lifeforms living on/in it. This is simply because technologies on Earth are still unable to detect or observe anything beyond the third dimensional physical lifeforms.

Furthermore, in most of their searches, scientists on Earth are mainly trying to look for planets that have certain conditions or characteristics that are similar to Earth because they think that only planets that have the same conditions or characteristics as Earth would be able to support intelligent lifeforms. Some third dimensional lifeforms in the Known Universe are actually like the third dimensional lifeforms on Earth which need water, food, and oxygen in order to survive while some other third dimensional lifeforms on/in other planets don't really need water, food, or oxygen in order to survive. They need something else instead. The second or third density entities need actual physical food in order to survive while the fourth density entities and higher are mainly surviving on energy, not the physical food. Therefore, using the same conditions and characteristics of Earth to search for possible intelligent lifeforms on/in other planets is unrealistic and unsuitable.

In any civilizations throughout the Goongverse, when technology development is more advanced than spiritual awareness, self-destruction usually occurs. It had happened to many civilizations on other planets in the Known Universe and it had happened to civilizations on Earth as well. The most recent civilization on Earth that has destroyed themself because of their spiritual awareness couldn't catch up with their technological advancement was the Atlantis. The split between the Africa continent and the South America continent was the result of the Atlantis testing their advanced and powerful weapons. It wasn't because of the

Earth plates were moving like what scientists on Earth believe. It's true that the earth plates are constantly moving, but for the split between the South America continent and the Africa continent, it was the result of advance technology and powerful weapon testing, not the result of the earth plates were moving.

The Asteroid Belt between Mars and Jupiter used to be a planet before it got blew up into pieces. That planet was known as planet Kong or planet Maldek to intelligent lifeforms in the Solar System. The last civilization living on planet Kong was the third density entities. They had very advanced technologies. Their technologies were super advanced and super powerful, but their spiritual awareness was very low. They got affected heavily by the negative energy from the Anti Creator. Majority of them polarized negatively. They went to war with many neighboring planets; they didn't pursue peace and harmony. As the result, their planet got blew up into pieces because of their advanced and powerful weapon testing. Some teaching on Earth believes that it got blew up because of the neighboring planets, some even believe that the Galactic Council in charge of keeping peace in the Solar System decided to blow it up in order to end the violence that was spreading in the Solar System. This is misleading because one of the main goals of the Galactic Council is to keep peace between intelligent lifeforms in the Known Universe without using any violences interfering with any processes of solving any conflicts across the Known Universe. At this current spacetime, there are intelligent lifeforms living on/in every planet and every moon in the Solar System except the asteroid belt between Mars and Jupiter because it got blew up into pieces and it's currently under going through the healing and resetting process.

In the Solar System, the Sun is the entity that supports the highest intelligent lifeforms. The entities residing on/in the Sun are mainly the sixth density entities. To the third density entities on Earth, it's impossible for any living lifeforms to survive or live on/in the Sun because it's too hot, if anything gets close enough to it, it would get burnt and turn into ashes. That's only true for the lower density entities in the physical plane. The environment of the Sun is only suitable for supporting the entities with high vibrational frequencies, not for supporting the entities with low vibrational frequencies in the physical plane. To scientists on Earth, the Sun is constantly burning or glowing because of the nuclear fusion of hydrogen to helium is taking place in its core. However, the burning or nuclear fusion of hydrogen to helium in the core of the Sun is actually the energies and frequencies that the sixth density entities radiant out. Those are the radiant of life. Without the radiant of life producing by the sixth density entities from the Sun, many lifeforms in the lower dimensions in the Solar System wouldn't have existed. This applies to all lifeforms in the lower dimensions throughout the Known Universe and other Universes. The radiant of life from the higher dimensions make life possible for the lower dimensions. The sixth density entities are capable of creating energies and frequencies that can sustain life in the lower dimensions. Sometimes, there are conflicts between the sixth positive polarized density entities and the sixth negative polarized density entities on/in the Sun which causes unbalance to the radiant of life. Scientists on Earth called the unbalanced radiant of life as solar flares. Severe solar flares can take away many lifeforms in the lower dimensions on/in the planets nearby. The sixth positive polarized density entities on/in the Sun are the entities that in charge of keeping the conflict with the sixth negative polarized density entities to the minimum to avoid any destructions to the lifeforms in the lower dimensions on/in the planets nearby.

One day when the Sun raises up its vibrational frequencies, it would be able to support the seventh dimensional lifeforms. For that to happen, the Sun would have to go through a major transition such as an explosion, after the explosion, the Sun would eventually transition to become a white dwarf star and would be able to support the seventh dimensional lifeforms. Because the seventh density entities are mainly positive polarized entities, the energies and frequencies these entities emitting out from the white dwarf star are much more angelic and much more divine. When the seventh density entities on/in the white dwarf star have learned all of their cosmic lessons in the lower sub-dimensions of the seventh dimension and moved up to the highest sub-dimension of the seventh dimension, which is the 7.7 sub-dimension, they no longer emitting light that can be seen or detected by any technologies on Earth at this current spacetime. This is when the white dwarf star has transitioned to become a black dwarf star. There are still billions of earth years until the day the Sun would go through the transitioning process in order to support the seventh dimensional lifeforms. Scientists on Earth think of the transitioning process as if the Sun would explode and turn into a white dwarf star. To the higher density entities, it simply means that the Sun at that spacetime has risen up its vibrational frequencies and can support the highest lifeforms in the Known Universe. This transitioning process would consider as the graduation process of the sixth density entities. Whichever entities can make it to the graduation would move up to the seventh dimension where they would learn their final cosmic lessons in the Known Universe to prepare themselves to exit the Known Universe and move up to the Multiverse where the Known Universe is located. For that transition to happen, the Sun would need a few other planetary entities to join together to become one powerful entity. Mercury, Venus, Earth, Mars, Jupiter, Saturn, Uranus, and Neptune are the potential candidates that would join the Sun to become one powerful entity that can support the seventh dimensional lifeforms. The minimum requirement for the planetary entities to join the Sun to become one powerful entity is that the planetary entities must minimally vibrate in the frequencies of the highest sub-dimension of the sixth dimension and can support lifeforms from the fifth dimension up to the sixth dimension. When the transitioning process occurs, the ungraduated entities on those planets would be transported to other suitable planets in the Known

Universe for them to continue learning their cosmic lessons that they haven't finished learning. Transporting the fifth density entities or the sixth density entities to other planets is such an easy job and it can be done within just a few seconds of earth time. It wouldn't be a tedious process like transporting the third density entities on Earth or the third density entities on any other third dimensional planets in the physical plane in the Known Universe or in other Universes.

Mercury and Venus are capable of supporting the fourth and the fifth dimensional lifeforms at this current spacetime. Civilizations on/in Mercury and Venus have advanced themselves from the third dimension to the fourth dimension, then to the fifth dimension, moving from the physical plane to the lower astral plane. During each transition, there were entities left behind who couldn't make it to the graduation. They couldn't move up to the higher dimensions because they haven't finished learning all the cosmic lessons that they have to learn in order to graduate. The third density entities who couldn't graduate and move up to the fourth dimension on/in Mercury and Venus got transported to Earth for them to relearn their third dimensional cosmic lessons. The fourth density entities that couldn't graduate and move up to the fifth dimension actually have a chance to relearn their fourth dimensional cosmic lessons on/in Venus and Mercury since Venus and Mercury are still capable of supporting the fourth dimensional lifeforms. One day when the third density entities that got transported to Earth have learned all of their third dimensional cosmic lessons and have raised up their vibrational frequencies, they would be able to graduate and move up to the fourth dimension in the lower astral plane.

Jupiter and Saturn are mainly supporting the fourth and the fifth dimensional lifeforms at this current spacetime. Jupiter and Saturn are the capital of the Solar System where the peace keepers of the Solar System usually meet to discuss or make important decisions regarding the process of keeping peace and harmony within the Solar System. Members of the Peace Keeper group in the Solar System comprises of the fifth and the sixth density entities. The peace keeper group is working under the guidance of the Galactic Council and responsible for carrying out any missions that assigned by the Galactic Council or solving any conflicts between any intelligent lifeforms in the Solar System.

Mars is currently finishing the transitioning process of moving from the third dimension up to the fourth dimension. Mars is mainly supporting the fourth dimensional lifeforms at this current spacetime. Like Venus, during the transitioning process from the third dimension to the fourth dimension, many entities couldn't make it to the graduation. They haven't finished learning their third dimensional cosmic lessons and they haven't risen up their vibrational frequencies to the vibrational frequencies of the fourth dimension, therefore, they couldn't graduate and move up to the fourth dimension. The ungraduated third density entities on Mars got transported to Earth for them to relearn their third dimensional cosmic lessons like those ungraduated third density entities from Venus and Mercury. Many third density entities from Mars, Mercury, and Venus are here on Earth at this current spacetime.

Earth is currently going through the transitioning process of supporting the third dimensional lifeforms to the fourth dimensional lifeforms. At this current spacetime, Earth is mainly supporting lifeforms from the first dimension up to the third dimension. The process of transitioning to support the fourth dimensional lifeforms is a difficult transition for Earth since many third density entities residing on Earth at this current spacetime have been on Earth for too long and have gone through so many incarnations on Earth without being able to wake up to learn their third dimensional cosmic lessons. Each time when they reincarnate back to Earth, they have to pass through the cosmic veil of forgetfulness. That makes them completely forget about their previous identities. They don't know who they are and what they are here on Earth for. Besides that, most of the third density entities on Earth at this current spacetime are actually not originated from the same region of the Known Universe. This is one of the reasons that creates many conflicts between the third density entity groups on Earth. The origins of the third density entities in the Known Universe also make it difficult for the transitioning since the third density entities in the Known Universe are not originated from the same Universe. Another reason that makes it difficult for the transitioning from the third dimension to the fourth dimension is that many of the third density entities on Earth at this current spacetime are still struggling with the cosmic traumas that they had experienced from their previous incarnations on their previous home planets before they got transported to Earth such as the third density entities from planet Kong. This makes it very hard for them to learn their third dimensional cosmic lessons on Earth since their souls are still going through the healing process. Therefore, the transition from the third dimension to the fourth dimension on Earth at this current spacetime is very difficult.

Center of the Milky Way galaxy is home to many seventh density entities. These seventh density entities are the entities from the higher sub-dimensions of the seventh dimension. Some entities no longer emitting light that can be seen or detected by any technologies on Earth at this current spacetime. When the seventh density entities go through the graduation process to exit the Known Universe, they can emit the strongest and brightest light that even outshines the entire light of their host galaxy and can be seen or detected from billions of light years away. Like the Milky Way galaxy, centers of other galaxies in the Known Universe and in other Universes are also home to many seventh density entities. The brightest objects in the Known Universe which are known to scientists on Earth as Quasars are actually the lights that emitted out by the seventh density entities when they go through the graduation process from exiting the Known Universe and move up to the Multiverse where the

Known Universe is located. The brightness level of each Quasar depends on the number of the seventh density entities who make it to the graduation in that particular graduation period. Normally Quasars are always more than 100 times brighter than the light of the galaxies which host them. Sometimes, some Quasars are 1000 times brighter than the light of the galaxies that host them because of the massive amount of light that got emitted out by a large number of the seventh density entities who are undergoing through the graduation process. Quasar emission usually lasts until the graduation process is completed. The duration of the graduation for the seventh density entities to graduate and move up to the Multiverse where their host Universe is located is around 100 million to 1000 million earth years. Sometimes it can be a bit longer or a bit shorter. Therefore, lifecycle of each quasar usually ranging from 100 million to 1000 million earth years. Sometimes it can be a bit longer or a bit shorter.

# Chapter 5

# Origins of the Third Density Entities on Earth

Scientists on Earth keep searching for the answers to the origins of the third density entities here on Earth, however, if they don't broaden and expand their searches into outer space, they won't be able to find the answer to human origins or the third density entity origins. Scientists and the third density entities on Earth keep searching for evidence of extraterrestrials here on Earth while they are actually the extraterrestrials. The third density entities on Earth aren't native to Earth. They originated from every corner of the Known Universe. Many civilizations from different planets across the Known Universe went through the transitioning process from the third dimension to the fourth dimension, when the transitioning process completed, many third density entities from their planets couldn't make it to the graduation because they haven't finished learning their third dimensional cosmic lessons while their home planets already risen up its vibrational frequencies and no longer supporting the third dimensional lifeforms. The third density entities who couldn't graduate and move up to the fourth dimension like the rest of the population on their planets needed a new third dimensional school for them to relearn their third dimensional cosmic lessons again so they can prepare themselves to graduate and move up to the fourth dimension. The ungraduated third density entities got transported to Earth for them to relearn their third dimensional cosmic lessons. At this current spacetime, Earth is the third dimensional school in the Known Universe that has the third dimensional students originated from almost every corner of the Known Universe. This is why so many conflicts between human races here on Earth can't be resolved easily using diplomatic solutions. Besides that, the origins of the third density entities in the Known Universe also makes it harder for them to get along here on Earth. All lifeforms in the Known Universe including the third density entities in the Known Universe originated from three different Universes. These three Universes no longer exist at this current spacetime. (This cosmic event will be explained more in later chapter of this book). Too many differences in their origins, backgrounds, cultures, behaviors, cosmic karmas, and the way each group think or behave make it difficult for the third density entities on Earth to solve any conflicts diplomatically.

Many ungraduated third density entities in the Known Universe have been transferring around to different third dimensional schools in different galaxies for them to relearn their third dimensional cosmic lessons. The third density entities from older galaxies or older star systems who couldn't make it to the graduation and move up to the fourth dimension got transported to younger or newly formed galaxies or star systems which still supporting the third dimensional lifeforms for them to continue learning their third dimensional cosmic lessons. Many third density entities in the Milky Way galaxy got transported from other older galaxies which no longer supporting the third dimensional lifeforms such as galaxies known to scientists on Earth as the GLASS-z13 galaxy and the GN-z11 galaxy. One day when the Milky Way galaxy no longer supporting the third dimensional lifeforms, any third density entities who couldn't make it to the graduation at that spacetime would be transported to other younger and newly formed galaxies which still supporting the third dimensional lifeforms for them to relearn their third dimensional cosmic lessons. The third density entities in the Solar System where Earth is located originally came from other older star systems in the Milky Way Galaxies and other Galaxies. When an older star system has advanced itself to support higher dimensional lifeforms and no longer supporting the third dimensional lifeforms, the ungraduated third density entities in that particular star system got transported to a younger and newly formed star system for them to relearn their cosmic lessons. The Solar System is considered a very young and newly formed star system in the Milky Way galaxy, therefore, many ungraduated third density entities from other older star systems got transported to the Solar System for them to relearn their third dimensional cosmic lessons. Many third density entities after got transported to the Solar System, they have learned their third dimensional cosmic lessons and have moved up to the fourth and the fifth dimension on Mercury, Venus, Mars, Saturn, Jupiter and Neptune. The third density entities who couldn't make it to the graduation on Mercury, Venus, Mars, Jupiter, Saturn, or Neptune got transported to Earth for them to relearn their third dimensional cosmic lessons. At this current space time, planets that can offer the third dimensional cosmic lessons in the Known Universe become lesser and lesser and overcrowded. This is because many third density entities failed to learn their third dimensional cosmic lessons on their home planets and their home planets have already advanced themselves to support higher dimensional lifeforms. That's why many ungraduated third density entities from other star systems in other galaxies also got transported to Earth and other third dimensional planets in the Milky Way galaxy for them to relearn their third dimensional cosmic lessons since they no longer have the third dimensional schools in their galaxies or star systems to send them to.

Eons ago, Earth started to receive those first ungraduated third density entities. They got transported to Earth in two ways. The first way was through spaceships and the second way was through soul transport. The entities that got transported to Earth through spaceships didn't have to go through the dying process and leave their physical bodies behind on their planets in order to come to Earth. They arrived to Earth through spaceship and settled down in different regions of the Earth. Before their arrival, there were only first and second density entities residing on Earth. This is why in the evolution theory on Earth, scientists still cannot find the missing link that initiated the jump from the second density entities to the third density entities on Earth.

The third density entities who came to Earth through spaceships also brought many first and second density entities from their home planets with them. That's why even some trees and animals on planet Earth at this current spacetime are not originated from Earth but from other planets. Many ungraduated third density entities from Pleiades, Alpha Centauri, Venus, Mercury, etc. got transported to Earth through spaceships. When those entities landed here on Earth, they started to reproduce and build societies. Afterwards, many ungraduated third density entities from many other planets across the Known Universe got transported to Earth slowly through soul transport. The entities that got transported to Earth through soul transport had to go through the dying process. They had to leave their physical bodies behind on their home planets, only their souls got transported to Earth through incarnation. They used the bodies of the offsprings produced by the third density groups that got transported to Earth earlier through spaceships as their third dimensional physical bodies. For the entities that came to Earth through soul transport, their souls must pass through the cosmic veil of forgetfulness. When they passed through the cosmic veil of forgetfulness, they forgot all about their memories, identities, and past life experiences from their home planets. They started their new lives here on Earth without remembering who they were in their previous lives, or where they originally came from. The entities that got transported to Earth through spaceships have taught the entities who came later to Earth through soul transport about their origins, but as time passed by, and as the older generation who came to Earth through spaceships ended their first lifecycle here on Earth, their souls went through the reincarnation wheel in order for them to come back to Earth to relearn their third dimensional cosmic lessons again. When they reincarnated back to Earth, they had to go through the cosmic veil of forgetfulness. This made them forgot about their previous life experiences, they forgot who they were or where they originally came from. As time passed by, whatever taught by the older generation who first came to Earth through spaceships about human origins became forgotten. The origins of human which originally came to Earth from outer space remain as something fictional, mysterious, and imaginative to the third density entities on Earth.

The third density entities on Earth originally had 13 strands of DNA and 100% of their brains were in full capacity. Of the 13 strands of DNA, 3 of them were single-stranded DNA and 10 of them were double-stranded DNA. They could live up to 1000 earth years. They were about twelve times stronger than the current third density entities (the modern human race). The graduation period was set to be every 200 thousand earth years. This means that every 200 thousand earth years, there would be one graduation taking place on Earth for the third density entities to graduate. Any third density entities who have learned all of their third dimensional cosmic lessons, which are the lessons of love and compassion, be able to vibrate in higher vibrational frequencies and be able to let go all of the attachments here on Earth would be able to graduate and move up to the fourth dimension. However, after 200 thousand earth years of being sent to Earth and many entities got reincarnated on Earth to relearn their third dimensional cosmic lessons several times, none of the third density entities could make it to the graduation. It was the same for the second and the third graduation cycle. None of the third density entities could make it to the graduation. During those 600 thousand earth years, they were too busy building societies, established ownerships, each individual was only interested in doing things that would benefit himself or herself. One group was trying to claim power over the other groups. War and killing happened constantly during that spacetime. Earth was nearly got destroyed because of their advanced technologies and powerful weapons. The Universal Council and the Galactic Council saw interference was needed. They gathered an emergency meeting on Saturn regarding the unsettling matters of the third density entities on Earth. They decided to do some genetic alterations to the physical bodies of the third density entities on Earth. They wanted to give the third density entities a higher chance of learning their third dimensional cosmic lessons without being able to develop any advanced technologies or weapons that could destroy Earth before they could make it to the graduation. The

Universal Council no longer allowed the third density entities on Earth to have 13 strands of DNA and 100% of their brains in full capacity. They realized that with 13 strands of DNA and 100% of their brains in full capacity, the third density entities on Earth would be too powerful. They could build advanced weapons that could destroy Earth in very short period of time. The percentage of them could destroy Earth before they could make it to the graduation was very high. Therefore, the Universal Council decided to reduce the strands of their DNA and reduce the capacity of their brains. The Galactic Council is the group that in charge of carrying out the genetic alteration. They started to experiment with the genetic alterations for the third density entities on Earth.

At the first genetic alteration, the Galactic Council decided to reduce the DNA of the third density entities from 13 strands to 10 strands with the brain capacity of 90%. The 3 single-stranded DNA got removed from the third density entities on Earth completely. The third density entities became a bit weaker, lifespan got a bit shorter as compared to their ancestors, but they were still exceptionally powerful, they were still capable of developing advanced weapons that could destroy Earth in such a short period of time. The Universal Council and the Galactic Council weren't satisfied with the results; they decided to do the genetic alterations again. This time they reduced the DNA of the third density entities from 10 strands to 8 strands with the brain capacity of 80%. They also reduced the graduation time from every

200 thousand earth years to every 150 thousand earth years since the average lifespan of the third density entities on Earth got reduced after the genetic alterations. The average lifespan of the third density entities at that time was about 500 to 550 earth years. After the 150 thousand earth years, none of the third density entities on Earth could make it to the graduation. It was the same for the second and the third graduation cycles. During those 450 thousand earth years, not only they didn't learn the third dimensional cosmic core lessons, which are the lessons of love and compassion, but they also turned Earth to become a nuclear battle field. In many parts of the Earth today, scientists would still be able to detect the radiation left behind from the past in those nuclear battle fields. Those nuclear battle fields weren't because of the results of wars between alien species that took place on Earth or the war of the fourth density entities that took place on Earth, but because of the wars between the Earthlings themselves. The Universal Council and the Galactic Council decided to do the genetic alterations for the third time. This time they reduced the DNA of the third density entities from 8 strands to 6 strands with the brain capacity of 70%. The average lifespan of the third density entities on Earth got reduced to about 350 earth years. They also reduced the graduation cycle from every 150 thousand earth years to every 100 thousand earth years. After 100 thousand earth years, none of the third density entities on Earth could make it to the graduation. It was the same for the second and the third graduation cycles. None of the third density entities could make it to the graduation. During those

300 thousand earth years, they were too busy focusing on developing technologies and weapons for going to war against one another, claiming territories and establishing borders between groups. By the end of the 300 thousand earth years, the third density entities on Earth not only haven't learned the third dimensional cosmic core lessons, which are the lessons of love and compassion, but they also managed to get themselves almost close to extinction. The Universal Council and the Galactic Council decided to do the genetic alterations for the fourth time. This time they reduced the third density entities DNA from 6 strands to 4 strands with the brain capacity of 60%. The average lifespan of the third density entities on Earth got reduced to about 200 earth years. Since they got sent to Earth for too long, plus every time when they finished one incarnation on Earth, their souls went to the lower astral plane located between the third and the fourth dimension and got sent back to Earth for their next incarnation, each time they got sent back, they had to go through the cosmic veil of forgetfulness, therefore, they completely forgot who they were or where they originally came from. They also lost so much of their abilities to connect and communicate with the Known Universe after gone through so many genetic alterations. Each time when they went through one genetic alteration, they lose a great deal of their abilities. Many of their divine abilities got lost. They could hear less, see less, and communicate less with the Known Universe and the higher dimensions. The story of them originally came to Earth from outer space also no longer being told for hundred thousand of earth years. They

thought they originated from Earth. They started to get curious about the outer space and what's out there beyond planet Earth. They started to spend time and resources in developing technologies to explore the outer space rather than focusing on spiritual awakening or learning the cosmic lessons of love and compassion. Many spaceships and signals got sent to the outer space. This caught the attention of some negative polarized entities from the sixth dimension on/in the Orion Constellation. Those sixth negative polarized entities started to develop interest about Earth. They started to find a way to sneak into Earth despite this was against the rules of the Universal Council. The sixth negative polarized entities wanted to turn all the third density entities on Earth to polarize negatively. This would turn Earth to become a food bank for them since the main food of the negative polarized entities is the negative energy producing by any other negative entities in the lower dimensions. They want to keep the third density entities from graduating and move up to the fourth dimension as positive polarized entities, instead they want the third density entities to graduate and move up to the fourth dimension as negative polarized entities. The Universal Council and the Galactic Council saw the complications on Earth since they couldn't stop those sixth negative polarized density entities from interfering with the soul development processes of the third density entities on Earth, they decided to give the third density entities on Earth one of the most powerful cosmic protection charms that ever existed in the Known Universe, the protection charm that not even the members of the

Universal Council or the members of the Galactic Council or any negative polarized entities from the fourth, fifth, or sixth dimensions can control. That protection charm is the human freewill. They also decided to reduce the human DNA from 4 strands to 2 strands with the brain capacity of 50%. They also reduced the graduation cycle from every 100 thousand earth years to every 75 thousand earth years. The average lifespan of the third density entities on Earth got reduced to about 100 earth years. The Universal Council and the Galactic Council thought that by shortening the lifespan of the third density entities on Earth in each incarnation can greatly increase the number of times an entity can reincarnate back to Earth to relearn their cosmic lessons if he or she failed to learn the cosmic lessons in his or her previous incarnations, therefore, it would increase the chance for the third density entities on Earth to make it to the graduation in a shorter period of time.

By reducing the DNA of the third density entities from 13 strands to 2 strands, this made the third density entities on Earth lose almost all of their abilities to communicate with the higher dimensions in the Known Universe. They also lose great abilities to hear and to see. This made the third density entities on Earth appear as if they are the deaf and the blind entities in the Known Universe. As the third density entities no longer as powerful and as capable as their ancestors in the past. The Universal Council and the Galactic Council hope that they would spend more time focusing on spiritual awakening, learning their third dimensional cosmic lessons so they can graduate and move up to the fourth dimension before they can develop any advanced weapons or technologies which could lead themselves to extinction or destroying Earth. The third density entities are weak and fragile in their physical bodies now as compared to their ancestors in the past, they aren't as intelligent or as powerful, but they possess one of the most powerful protection charms in the Known Universe, the human freewill. With this protection charm, the negative polarized entities from the higher dimensions can't manipulate or interfere without the permission of the third density entities on Earth. The negative polarized entities from the higher dimensions can try to interfere, manipulate, or control the third density entities on Earth, but as long as the third density entities don't allow them to, there's nothing the negative polarized entities from the higher dimensions can do about it. They can try to continue to break the human free will. Certain individuals might give up and let the negative polarized entities get control over, but as soon as the third density entities change their minds and no longer allowing it, the negative polarized entities would lose their control over those certain individuals immediately. With the human freewill, not even the positive polarized entities from the higher dimensions can control or manipulate the third density entities on Earth. Manipulation or controlling only occurs when the third density entities on Earth allowing it to happen. The third density entities on Earth are now carrying one of the most powerful cosmic protection charms in the

Known Universe, however, many of them aren't aware of it and many of them have never put it into use.

On the two strands of the human DNA, scientists on Earth so far only be able to understand 1.5% of it. That's why they believe that only 1.5% of the human DNA are being active and 98.5% of the human DNA are inactive. Scientists on Earth classified those 98.5% of human DNA as junk DNA. The 98.5% of human DNA that scientists on Earth classified as junk DNA and have no clues about are actually not junk DNA, those are the main keys that leads to the spiritual awakening, connecting and communicating with the higher dimensions throughout the Known Universe. Scientific knowledges and technologies on Earth are not capable of observing, understanding, or measuring the activities of those 98.5% of human DNA yet.

Despite the fact that the third density entities on Earth only have two strands of DNA and could live up to only 100 earth years in each incarnation, some civilizations have been able to develop advanced technologies that surpassed their spiritual awareness. Since the last genetic alteration occurred, the third density entities on Earth have already gone through two graduation cycles. In those two graduation cycles, none of the third density entities could make it to the graduation. All of the entities that got qualified to move up to the higher dimensions in those two graduation cycles were the cosmic workers from the higher dimensions in the Known Universe who volunteered to come to Earth to help the third density entities with their cosmic lessons, not the ungraduated third density entities that got transported to Earth.

The third density entities on Earth are now entering the third graduation cycle since the last genetic alteration. During the last 75 thousand earth years in the third graduation cycle, some civilizations on Earth were able to develop advanced technologies and weapons that ended up leading their whole civilizations to destruction. The Atlantis civilization is one example. About 225 thousand earth years have passed since the last genetic alteration, the third density entities on Earth are now in the duration of the third graduation cycle. Earth has started to enter the graduation period for the third graduation cycle since the year of 2021. The duration of the graduation is about 50 earth years. By the year of 2071, the duration of the graduation for the third graduation cycle would be ended. The duration of the graduation can also be ended one year earlier or one year later in the 50 earth years duration. This means that the duration of the graduation can be ended in either the year of 2070, 2071 or 2072. The Universal Council and the Galactic Council are now watching the third graduation cycle of the third density entities on Earth very closely.

# Chapter 6

# The Cosmic workers

Since the third density entities on Earth have lost almost all of their abilities to communicate with the higher dimensions in the Known Universe, many signals got sent to Earth from the higher dimensions in the Known Universe to assist with the spiritual awakening process can't be received. With little of hearing, seeing, and communicating abilities left, the third density entities on Earth are not capable of hearing or receiving any signals from the higher dimensions. They have to spend time focusing and mastering their hearing and communicating skills with the higher dimensions in the Known Universe in order for them to be able to receive any signals. Since the third density entities spend most of their time focusing on building wealth to make their lives more comfortable while they are here on Earth, they barely spend their time focusing on mastering their communication skills with the Known Universe, therefore, they can't communicate or receive any assisting signals from the higher dimensions in the Known Universe. They are deep asleep here on Earth. The third density entities not only deep asleep but they also possess one of the most powerful cosmic protection charms in the Known Universe which none of the entities from the higher dimensions can manipulate or interfere without their freewill, that's why sending out signals to assist with the awakening process from the higher dimensions telepathically is impossible. Since sending help telepathically to assist the third density entities with their graduation is impossible, the Universal Council and the Galactic Council decided to send out cosmic volunteer workers to help the third density entities on Earth with their spiritual awakening process so they can learn their third dimensional cosmic lessons. Cosmic workers who volunteered or got assigned to help the third density entities on Earth must come to Earth through soul transport. They must pass through the cosmic veil of forgetfulness and enter Earth like any other third density entities who got sent to Earth through soul transport. They are not allowed to enter Earth as the higher density entities who still carrying all the cosmic power from the higher dimensions. If they come to Earth like that, the third density entities on Earth would instantly turn to worshiping them as Gods or the Infinite Creator. When they come to Earth through soul transport, they have to go through the awakening process in order for them to start doing their works. Once they are awakened, they would be able to show the third density entities on Earth the ways that lead to spiritual awakening. When the third density entities on Earth finally awakened, they can start learning their third dimensional cosmic lessons so they can graduate from the third dimension and move up to the fourth dimension.

Many cosmic workers had volunteered to come to Earth to help with the spiritual awakening in the long distance past, but the third density entities on Earth turned to worshiping them as Gods or the son of God. They built temples, churches, and created many religions out of those cosmic workers' teachings. One very well-known cosmic worker who volunteered on Earth in the long distance past and got worshiped by the third density entities on Earth like God or the son of God was Jesus. Jesus came to Earth, passed through the cosmic veil of forgetfulness, forgot all about his previous life and his identity in the higher dimension. He was born on Earth like any other third density entities. Eventually he was able to remember who he really was and the mission he had signed up for before coming to Earth. He started to plant the seed of awakening in the third density entities on Earth through his teachings. The third density entities on Earth mistakenly thought of him as God or the son of God. They turned to worshipping him. Jesus came from the highest sub-dimension of the fifth dimension. The fifth dimension is the dimension where the cosmic entities mainly focusing on gaining wisdom, knowledge, and balancing out between wisdom, knowledge, and love. Most cosmic workers come from the fifth dimension mainly focusing on teaching the third density entities on Earth about love, wisdom, and compassion. They don't focus on personal love life or want to get married or have children while they are volunteering here on Earth. Jesus' mission on Earth got terminated earlier than expected because of the interferences of the negative polarized entities from the higher dimensions. (While many cosmic workers got sent to Earth by the Universal Council and the Galactic Council, the negative polarized entities from the sixth dimension on/in the Orion Belt Constellation also sent out their volunteers to Earth to interfere with the missions of the cosmic workers and to turn the third density entities on Earth to polarize negatively). Despite that Jesus mission got terminated earlier than expected, he left many of his valuable teachings behind for the third density entities on Earth. Many of his teachings got manipulated by the third density entities on Earth to gain power and to control over large groups of crowds. Many churches got built on Earth to worship Jesus and God while Jesus himself didn't mention about building any churches or worshiping him as the son of God in his teachings. One of Jesus' most powerful teachings on Earth is: "I am the way and the truth and the life. No one comes to the Father except through me." If any third density entities on Earth get the message in this teaching right, they would be in the right path to their spiritual awakening. Unfortunately, many third density entities on Earth interpreted this message wrongly. The message in this teaching is that the only way to reach to the higher dimension where the Father or the Creator resides, the third density entities must be awakened, remember who they really are and what they are here on Earth for, do whatever they need to do here on Earth so they can go up to the higher dimensions, just like how he did it. Jesus came to Earth, remembered who he was, focusing on finishing the mission he had signed up for on Earth and went back to the higher dimension where he originally came from. That's the only way to go up to the higher dimension where the Father or the Creator resides, there is no other way. The higher dimension in here means the seventh dimension in the Known Universe since Jesus only has knowledge limited to the highest dimension of the Known Universe like any other entities in the Known Universe. Therefore, the seventh dimension would be the dimension where he thought the Father or the Creator would reside. Even though Jesus' mission got terminated earlier than expected, he had finished whatever he had signed up for on Earth. He had planted the seed of awakening in many third density entities on Earth. After his mission got terminated, Jesus went back to the highest sub-dimension of the fifth dimension and earned his way to the graduation, he graduated from the fifth dimension and moved up to the sixth dimension, the dimension of balancing between love and wisdom combined. Up until this current spacetime, Jesus hasn't expressed any desire of volunteering back to Earth physically to help the third density entities again. The Universal Council and the Galactic Council don't know if in the distance future, Jesus would want to volunteer to come back to Earth physically again or just helping the third density entities on Earth telepathically like what he is doing now while he is in the sixth dimension learning his sixth dimensional cosmic lessons.

Many cosmic workers from planets that have the ungraduated third density entities that got transported to Earth had volunteered to Earth in the distant past. The cosmic workers from Venus had been actively volunteering on Earth since the beginning. They had come and gone many times throughout Earth's history. They had taught the third density entities on Earth so much knowledge about the Known Universe, the Solar System, and particularly knowledge about planet Venus. Like any other entities in the Known Universe, cosmic workers from Venus only have knowledge limited to the Known Universe. They have no idea what's beyond the Known Universe or any other Universes besides the Known Universe. Anything beyond the Known Universe is inaccessible to them. Therefore, they think that the seventh dimension in the Known Universe is the highest dimension in the cosmos where the Infinite Creator would be residing. Cosmic workers from Venus had taught the third density entities on Earth to construct certain objects that can harness energy from the Solar System and nearby star systems. A few of them still can be found on Earth at this current spacetime. The pyramids and the Mayan temples are a few of them. So much knowledge about the Known Universe, the Solar System, and planet Venus had been given to the third density entities on Earth by the Venusian cosmic workers and had been written down and stored in a library on Earth in the recent past by a group of third density entities on Earth known as the Mayan. However, because of wars, conflicts, lack of knowledge, and limitations in understanding of other third density groups, the library got destroyed. When the third density group from the Europe continent arrived to the America continent and gained access to the library, they thought that the Mayan group was worshipping the devil because they couldn't understand the knowledge that was written in those books. They decided to burn down the whole library. A sea of knowledge about the Known Universe, the Solar System and planet Venus that had been given to the third density entities on Earth got lost. Most of the valuable Venusian teachings got removed from Earth's history up until this current spacetime. A few entities which known to the third density entities on Earth as priests or monks were the guardians of the library. They were able to grasp some books and fled out of the library. Only a few of those books got found and decoded by scientists on Earth in recent spacetime. However, those aren't the books that contain the most valuable teachings of the Venusian cosmic workers.

It wasn't easy for any cosmic workers to do their job here on Earth in the past. Any third density groups that the cosmic workers came to contact with and taught, they all ended up worshipping the cosmic workers as Gods. The Mayan group was no different, they also worshipped the Venusian cosmic workers as Gods. When the Venusian cosmic workers left, the Mayan group was desperate for their Gods to return, they did so many rituals out of desperation including sacrificing rituals with the hope that those rituals and sacrifices would please their Gods and their Gods would return. The Venusian cosmic workers had stopped their volunteering services on Earth for a short period of time after leaving behind so much cosmic knowledge to the Mayan group, the Amazon group, and the Egyptian group on Earth. Recently, when Earth was about to enter the graduation period of the third graduation cycle since the last genetic alteration, they started to offer assistance to Earth telepathically and physically again. There's one well known cosmic worker from Venus who has made significant impact on the soul development processes of the third density entities on Earth recently. That entity is Ra. Like any other cosmic workers from Venus, Ra only has information and knowledge of the seven dimensions in the Known Universe. Ra doesn't have access to any information beyond the Known Universe yet, therefore, in his teachings, the seventh dimension in the Known Universe is considered the highest dimension in the Cosmos. There aren't any other dimensions exist beyond the seventh dimension in his teaching on Earth. After offering his volunteering services to Earth, Ra has made his way to the graduation. He has just graduated from the fifth dimension and moved up to the sixth dimension where he would learn his sixth dimensional cosmic lessons to prepare himself for graduating and moving up to the seventh dimension. Ra is currently residing on the Sun; he's no longer residing on Venus.

Besides a large number of cosmic workers from Venus volunteering on Earth in the past, significant numbers of cosmic workers from the Pleiades, Alpha Centauri, Mars, Saturn, Arcturus, LMC dwarf galaxy, Andromeda galaxy, Pinwheel galaxy, and many other places in the Known Universe had volunteered on Earth in the past as well. They had tried to help the third density entities on Earth to reconnect with the higher dimensions and reconnect to their origins before they got transported to Earth. The cosmic workers had tried their best to help the third density entities on Earth with their awakening process. They were hoping that when the third density entities on Earth finally awakened, they would be able to remember who they are and what they are here on Earth for. They would start focusing on learning their third dimensional cosmic lessons and do whatever they need to do here on Earth in order for them to graduate and move up to the fourth dimension in the lower astral plane.

Despite the fact that there were many cosmic workers volunteering on Earth to help the third density entities since the last genetic alteration from the Universal Council and the Galactic Council, so far none of the ungraduated third density entities that got transported to Earth to learn their third dimensional cosmic lessons have made their way to the graduation in the past two graduation cycles since the last genetic alteration. The entities that could make it to the graduation and moved up to the higher dimensions in the past two graduation cycles were only the volunteer cosmic workers who had been awakened, not the ungraduated third density entities that got transported to Earth to relearn their third dimensional cosmic lessons. Not all of the cosmic workers who had been volunteering on Earth in the distant past could make their ways up to the higher dimensions where they originally came from, many of them are still here on Earth at this current spacetime. The reason why they are still here is because they got sucked into the dense third dimensional frequencies. They couldn't wake up and couldn't remember who they really are. They haven't done the jobs that they originally had signed up for before coming to Earth. Since they couldn't go back to the dimensions where they originally came from because they haven't been awakened, when they finished one incarnation here on Earth, they immediately got reincarnated and come back to Earth again like any other ungraduated third density entities. Many cosmic workers have been reincarnated back to Earth for hundreds of times already but still haven't been able to wake up to do their jobs yet. They have been sucked too deep into the dense third dimensional frequencies. They fell deep asleep. As long as they are still deep asleep and haven't been awakened, they won't be able to do their jobs and go back to the higher dimensions where they originally came from. They have to reincarnate here on Earth over and over again for hundreds or even thousands of earth years until they finally awakened. Maybe one day when they finally wake up from their deep sleep, they probably don't have to do their missions here on Earth anymore because their missions already get done by some other cosmic workers who volunteered to come to Earth after them. Nevertheless, they still need to wake up in order to go back to the higher dimensions where they originally came from.

To wake up those hundred or even thousand earth years sleeping cosmic workers is a difficult job for any awakened cosmic workers who are currently volunteering on Earth. Another catalyst that makes it difficult to wake up those deep asleep cosmic workers is that besides the positive polarized cosmic workers here on Earth from the Universal Council side, there are also the negative polarized entities from the Orion Constellation who have been sneaking into Earth trying to stop and delaying the awakening process of the third density entities. Once these negative polarized entities awakened, they would try to create turbulence and chaos here on Earth as much as possible. They would also try to stop the awakening process of any cosmic workers from the Universal Council side. This makes it even more difficult to wake up those cosmic workers who have been deep asleep here on Earth for hundreds or even thousands of earth years through many incarnations.

For the cosmic workers who are currently under going through the awakening process, there are many ways to avoid being manipulated by the higher negative polarized density entities who have been awakened. The first way is to use the cosmic protection charm, which is the human freewill. The cosmic workers should never let any entities manipulate or force them into doing something that they don't want to do or their hearts don't feel right about it. The freewill protection charm not only given to the ungraduated third density entities on Earth, but also be given to any cosmic workers who volunteering on Earth. Even the negative polarized entities from the higher dimensions who have been sneaking into Earth through soul transport also be able to receive this protection charm as well.

The second way for the cosmic workers to avoid being manipulated by any higher negative polarized density entities who have been awakened is to radiant out their love, kindness, and light. The thing that the negative polarized entities afraid of the most in the Cosmos is love. Love can weaken and erase all the negative power that any negative polarized entities have. Love can convert any negative polarized entities into positive polarized entities. Just like in a dark room, when the light turns on, darkness will immediately disappear. So whenever being approached by a negative polarized entity, cosmic workers should send out their love, light, and kindness. The negative entities would afraid of losing their power and they might not even want to get close to the cosmic workers. If the cosmic workers send out angers or hatreds, that would only make the negative polarized entities become stronger since the negative polarized entities feed on negative energies. They can easily use the negative emotions to manipulate and to drain out the energy from the cosmic workers. At the end, when the cosmic workers become extremely exhausted, they might give up from being positive and slowly turn their feelings and thoughts into negative. This would make the cosmic workers slowly turn to polarize negatively.

The third way for the cosmic workers to avoid being manipulated by any higher negative polarized density entities who have been awakened is always be positive. When their thinkings and thoughts are positive, the negative entities have no chance of feeding them any negative thinkings or any negative thoughts. Everything in this third dimensional physical existence starts with a thought, then the thought being manifested and becomes a physical thing. So, keeping the thoughts and feelings positive not only can help the cosmic workers avoid being approached by any negative polarized entities, but also help them manifest and attract all the positive things into their lives while they are volunteering here on Earth. Because the Anti Creator is constantly infusing negative energy into every verse in the Goongverse, being positive can also help minimize the effects of the negative energy from the Anti Creator on the cosmic workers while they are in the awakening process to avoid being polarized negatively.

There had never been as many cosmic workers here on Earth as it is at this current spacetime. Out of the 8.3 billion third density entities here on Earth at this current spacetime, millions of them are cosmic workers. Many of them already awakened and are actively doing their jobs. Many are still deep asleep. The cosmic workers who are already awakened and are doing their jobs, they should know that the Universal Council and the Galactic Council are deeply appreciate their services and their sacrifices. The Universal Council and the Galactic Council can't wait to see them again in the higher dimensions when they have finished their missions here on Earth. For the cosmic workers who are still unawakened and have no clues about who they are or what they are here on Earth for, they shouldn't be worried, the awakening process can take time. They should let their souls go through all the necessary trainings, when they are ready, they will be awakened.

For the cosmic workers who haven't been awakened, they should try to spend more time meditating, observing things that happening around them and think of those things as clues or catalysts that are trying to wake them up or to ignite the awakening process in them. They should remember that they are not alone in their journeys, their higher selves and other entities from the higher dimensions are always ready to aid them whenever they ask for or whenever they need help the most. Chances are they're still deep asleep because they are the entities who carry very important cosmic missions here on Earth. Remember that cosmic workers who carry important missions here on Earth can be the entities that are in the deepest sleep when they got sent to Earth. This is because the cosmic workers who carry important missions here on Earth have to go through necessary trainings and experiences so they would be mature enough, wise enough, and mentally strong enough. When they start their awakening process, they cannot be manipulated easily by any higher negative polarized density entities or being affected by the negative energy that the Anti Creator constantly infusing into every verse in the Goongverse. Whenever a cosmic worker starts his or her awakening process, any awakened negative polarized entities on Earth can detect it telepathically. They would try their best to stop the awakening process, if they can't stop it, they would try to manipulate the awakening process to turn the cosmic worker into polarizing negatively. This is why the cosmic workers who carrying important missions here on Earth have been programmed to be deep asleep, they can only wake up when they are mentally and emotionally mature enough so they cannot be manipulated easily by any awakened negative polarized entities. The downside of this is that any cosmic workers who have been programmed to be deep asleep, once they incarnate here on Earth, they usually get sucked into the dense third dimensional frequencies and might never be able to wake up. Some cosmic workers have reincarnated many times on Earth but still haven't been able to wake up yet. The cosmic workers who haven't been awakened, when they finish one incarnation here on Earth, they would go up to the lower astral plane between the third and the fourth dimensions and get send back to Earth again like any other ungraduated third density entities. They might need to reincarnate hundreds or thousands of times here on Earth until they finally awakened so they can do their jobs and go back to the higher dimensions where they originally came from. This is the risk that any cosmic workers would have to take while volunteering here on Earth to help the ungraduated third density entities.

Another risk that any cosmic workers would have to take while volunteering on Earth or on any other planets in the physical planes is that they can turn to polarize negatively because of the negative energy that the Anti Creator constantly infusing into the Goongverse and the manipulation of the higher negative polarized density entities who have been awakened. If a cosmic worker wakes up and polarizes negatively in the third dimension and be able to graduate negatively all the way up to the highest sub-dimension of the sixth dimension, he or she would have to repeat the process again starting from the third dimension where he or she started to polarize negatively. In this situation, the cosmic worker would have to learn the third dimensional cosmic lessons like any ungraduated third density entities. His or her cosmic missions would be canceled. He or she would have to repeat the process over and over again until he or she turns to polarize positively all the way up to the seventh dimension since the negative polarized entities in the universal verse cannot graduate and move up to the multiversal verse.

Even though there are risks of not being able to wake up to do their jobs and go back to the higher dimensions while volunteering here on Earth and might have to reincarnate hundreds or even thousands of times on Earth like any ungraduated third density entities before being able to wake up to do their jobs and go back, the reward for volunteering on Earth is also very great. Volunteering on Earth or on any other third dimensional planets in the physical plane can significantly reduce the graduation time for any cosmic workers from the higher dimensions. When a cosmic worker finishes his or her missions here on Earth and goes back to the dimension where he or she originally came from, he or she can easily graduate and move up to the higher dimension beyond the dimension he or she originally came from. For example, in order to graduate from the fifth dimension and move up to the sixth dimension, it could take hundred million or even a billion earth years for the fifth density entities to learn the necessary cosmic lessons in order to graduate. However, for the cosmic workers who volunteered to help the ungraduated third density entities on Earth or on any other third dimensional planets in the physical plane, the graduation time can be reduced to a few million earth years instead. Reincarnating on Earth for thousands of earth years might sound like a very long time to the third density entities on Earth, however, because of the distortion of spacetime in different dimensions, one thousand earth years can be only one year in the fourth dimension, one month in the fifth dimension, one week in the sixth dimension and one day in the seventh dimension.

Because of the risk that many cosmic workers might not be able to wake up while volunteering here on Earth or might be awakened negatively because of the manipulation of the awakened negative polarized entities and the negative energy from the Anti Creator, the Universal Council and the Galactic Council decided to send a large number of cosmic workers to Earth at this current spacetime to help with the graduation process. Many cosmic workers come to Earth at this current spacetime carrying the same missions. If a few cosmic workers fail to wake up to do their jobs, there would be other cosmic workers who could wake up to carry out their missions for them. The reasons why a great number of cosmic workers got sent to Earth at this current spacetime is because Earth is entering the graduation period of the 75 thousand earth years graduation cycle. This graduation is the third graduation cycle on Earth since the last genetic alteration. The Universal Council, the Galactic Council, and the higher density entities are hoping that a great number of the third density entities would be able to make it to the graduation in this cycle, not like those previous graduation cycles that none of the ungraduated third density entities could make it to the graduation and move up to the fourth dimension.

Many seventh density entities are volunteering on Earth at this current spacetime. In the past, there weren't any entities from the seventh dimension volunteering here on Earth. At this current spacetime, there are some seventh density entities volunteering on Earth even come from the highest sub-dimension of the seventh dimension. Those are the entities who are in the process of learning their final cosmic lessons to prepare themselves to graduate and move up to the Multiverse. They wanted to volunteer physically in the physical plane one last time before they make their ways to the graduation so they can exit the Known Universe and move up to the Multiverse where the Known Universe is located. Once they move up to the Multiverse, they cannot volunteer physically in the physical plane in the Known Universe or in any other Universes anymore. If they ever volunteer to help the entities in the universal verse, it would be assisting the seventh density entities with their graduation process from the universal verse to the multiversal verse only. They can't assist the entities below the seventh dimension because of their high vibrational frequencies. The sixth density entities and lower can't access the assistance services that the eighth density entities provide telepathically to the universal verse. Only the seventh density entities who are about to graduate can access the assistance from the eighth density entities telepathically.

The entities from the highest sub-dimension of the seventh dimension are the entities that carrying very important missions here on Earth at this current spacetime for this graduation cycle. The highest seventh density entities once awakened, they would have the abilities to see other entities from different dimensions up until the seventh dimension. Besides helping the third density entities with their awakening process, the seventh density entities also in charge of helping the Earth raise up its vibrational frequencies. They are the main entities that holding the key in the process of shifting consciousness of planet Earth at this current spacetime. These seventh density entities once awakened, they can travel telepathically back and forth from Earth to other parts of the Known Universe in couple of milliseconds. The third density entities on Earth refers to this experience as out of body experience. Every cosmic worker on Earth experiences the out of body experience differently based on the dimension and sub-dimension they originally came from. Those came from the higher dimension or higher sub-dimension usually have greater abilities to travel further into space and can travel more often as compare to those cosmic workers came from lower dimension or lower sub-dimension. Traveling through space is an easy task for any entities starting from the fourth dimension and up. Any fourth density entities can travel from one planet to the next or from one star system to the next star system within couple of milliseconds. Any fifth density entities and sixth density entities can travel from one galaxy to the next galaxy within couple of milliseconds. Any seventh density entities can travel to anywhere in the Known Universe within couple of milliseconds. Scientists on Earth at this current spacetime still struggling with the idea of building spaceships that can travel at the speed of light. Traveling at the speed of light is an inadequate and incompetent way of traveling to other parts of the Known Universe. For the third density entities who are not capable of traveling telepathically within their host Universe yet, the best way for them to travel is traveling through space portals, not traveling through spaceships at the speed of light.

The main way for cosmic workers to come to Earth is through soul transport, which means they have to leave their divine astral bodies behind and use the third density entity bodies as their operating vehicles while volunteering here on Earth. They also have to pass through the cosmic veil of forgetfulness in order to come to Earth. They have to forget all about their memories and their identities from the higher dimensions. However, in rare situations, there are some cosmic workers who volunteering on Earth still be able to carry all the memories and identities of their previous lives from the higher dimensions because they don't have to go through the cosmic veil of forgetfulness in order to come to Earth. They don't come to Earth through soul transport, they come to Earth through a different path which is known as the walkin path. This way of volunteering is extremely rare and only happens when matters on Earth are extremely urgent. The walkin volunteers usually come quickly and go quickly once they get their jobs done. Since the walkin cosmic volunteers carry all the memories and knowledges of the higher dimensions, they remain very powerful even though they have to use the third density entity bodies as their operating vehicles while volunteering on Earth. They can manifest new third density entity bodies or they can temporarily borrow bodies from other third density entities while they are volunteering on Earth. Most of the time they just manifest new third density physical bodies. Borrowing bodies from other third density entities on Earth is extremely rare. Some entities on Earth have claimed that they are the walkin cosmic workers. However, walkin cosmic workers come and go quickly and they usually don't leave that many traces or clues behind when they get their jobs done here on Earth. Majority of the cosmic workers who claimed to be the walkin cosmic volunteers are actually the cosmic workers that came to Earth through soul transport. Because of certain incidents in their lives that ignited the seed of awakening in them, they become awakened and started to remember who they are and the missions they have signed up here on Earth.

When the cosmic workers from the higher dimensions volunteering on Earth, each of them leaves behind a fragment of their souls in the higher dimensions. These fragments of their souls have the mission of assisting and guiding the cosmic workers while they are here on Earth telepathically. These fragments of their souls are their higher selves. Only the cosmic workers who come to Earth through soul transport would leave behind a fragment of their souls in the higher dimensions in order to guide them. Cosmic workers who come to Earth through walkin don't leave behind any fragments of their souls in the higher dimensions since they don't have to pass through the cosmic veil of forgetfulness, they have the privilege of keeping all the cosmic memories from the higher dimensions while volunteering here on Earth. Cosmic workers on Earth don't have the ability to connect with their higher selves if they are still not in the process of awakening. However, their higher selves have always been watching them and protecting them since the first day they set their footsteps on Earth. Many of the higher selves even went extra miles to save the cosmic workers when they were in critical situations which could terminate their missions here on Earth early. Many cosmic workers got saved by their higher selves when they were about to get into a car accident or being shot at. With a blink of an eye, their higher selves appeared to steer the wheels or change the speed or change the direction of their cars or other cars, or to block the bullets from hitting the cosmic workers or to change the direction of the bullets. The higher selves play an important role in the process of waking up the cosmic workers while they are still deep asleep on Earth. The higher selves always try to send out signals and guidance to the cosmic workers through dreams and through other clues in their daily lives. The cosmic workers just have to pay close attention to their dreams in order to get messages from their higher selves. Observing all the things that happening in their daily lives can also help the cosmic workers find out the clues that are given to them by their higher selves to help with their awakening process or to help with their missions here on Earth.

Besides leaving a fragment of their souls in the higher dimension to act as the cosmic guides, each cosmic worker can split his or her soul in two halves to volunteer in two different planets in the physical plane. Half of his or her soul would be volunteering here on Earth, while the other half would be volunteering on a different planet in the Known Universe at the same spacetime. These two halves of the same soul are known as twin souls. Usually only cosmic workers who have their souls split in two halves to volunteer in two different planets in the physical plane would have twin souls. The ungraduated third density entities on Earth don't have twin souls. The lovers, spouses, or partners they have here on Earth are their soulmates, not their twin souls. Cosmic workers who have their twin souls volunteering on different planets can still have soulmates while they are volunteering on Earth. However, when it comes to twin soul, they only have one, which is the other half of the soul that got split from the same soul. Because of the strong bond and connection of the twin souls, some cosmic workers on Earth might not be able to accept any other entities on Earth as their soulmates while volunteering here on Earth. They constantly miss or long for someone that they don't even know who exactly that person is. Nothing on Earth can make them feel complete or fill in the void. Sometimes they might meet their twin souls in dreams but they might not even realize those are their twin souls. Meeting twin souls in dreams usually makes the cosmic workers feel very pleasant. The present of their twin souls in dreams make everything feel so complete, so perfect and so magnificent. Some cosmic workers might not even want to wake up from their magnificent dreams of meeting their twin souls. The cosmic workers who have their twin souls volunteering on other planets are the entities that have the hardest time adjusting to the ways of life here on Earth. They constantly feel they don't belong here and constantly have the feeling of wanting to go home when they don't even know exactly where their home is.

There are a great number of cosmic workers who are already awakened on Earth at this current spacetime but still haven't found out the purposes of their missions here on Earth yet. Majority of the cosmic workers come to Earth carrying the mission of sending out love, light, and positive energy while being here on Earth. Therefore, for the awakened cosmic workers who haven't found out the purposes of their missions here on Earth yet, maybe the main purpose of their missions here on Earth is to be positive so that they can send out love, light, and positive energy to the third density entities they come into contact with. Being positive can raise up the vibrational frequencies of the third density entities around them. Being positive can also raise up the vibrational frequencies of the Earth. When a great number of the cosmic workers are positive, the love, light, and positive energy they send out would have great positive impact on the third density entities here on Earth and have great positive impact on the planet itself as well.

Different cosmic workers might have different missions here on Earth, however, there's one mission that they all share, that mission is to remain positive. Some cosmic workers might come to Earth with the mission of waking up other sleeping cosmic workers. Some cosmic workers might come to Earth to write a book to spread knowledge about different dimensions of the Known Universe. Writing a book or create a channel preaching about knowledge of different dimensions in the Known Universe has great impact on the third density entities on Earth. It's like planting a seed of awakening inside each of the third density entities. However, for the seed of awakening to grow and flourish, it needs a positive surrounding and positive environment. Therefore, remaining positive after planting out the seed of awakening in the third density entities on Earth is important. It can make great positive impact on the third density entities in their awakening process as well as make great positive impact on the vibrational frequencies of the Earth.

Any cosmic workers who have been awakened would automatically unlock the cosmic creator power within them. They can start becoming the creators of their own lives here in the third dimension. The cosmic blue imprint that they carry with them when they incarnated here on Earth would disappear once they are awakened. There are no restrictions for what they can and cannot create. It's the same for any third density entities here on Earth to learn their third dimensional cosmic lessons. Once they are awakened, they can start becoming the creators of their own lives and their own realities here on Earth. Creating and manifesting reality at this current spacetime is easier than ever before because Earth has entered the graduation period of the third graduation cycle since the last genetic alteration since 2021. Whenever the third density entities on Earth entering the graduation period, so much help from the higher dimensions got sent to Earth. With the high level of energies and high vibrational frequencies presenting on Earth during this graduation period, manifesting for anything become much faster and much easier. Therefore, creating a desirable reality on Earth at this current spacetime is easier and faster than ever before.

For the cosmic workers or the third density entities on Earth at this current spacetime who constantly feel that they are having a hard time in life or they feel they are powerless to do anything to change their lives or their realities, the first thing they need to do is to change their perspectives. Perspectives are the glasses that the third density entities on

Earth wear to see the world. Some unawakened cosmic workers wear them to see the world as well. Perspectives can hold any entities back from doing things that they are capable of doing. Most of the time they are far more empowered in their lives than they could realize. Therefore, changing perspectives can change their lives. Changing perspectives can open up the doors to new opportunities and new possibilities. Things that they think impossible for them to achieve can be achieved very easily. Just like when reading this book, if an entity still sticking to the old perspectives of the Known Universe and only believe that the laws of physics in the Known Universe are the laws of physics that governing throughout the whole Cosmos, or everything must be proven by science or technologies on Earth in order for it to be true, then he or she must feel that this book is talking about nonsense or the writer of this book must be a crazy entity. But if he or she change his or her perspectives, believing that not everything in the vast Cosmos would follow the same laws of physics that the Known Universe is operating on or the current technologies on Earth are not capable of seeing or detecting any lifeforms beyond the third dimension or capable of seeing or detecting anything beyond the Observable Universe, then he or she would start opening the door to receive new knowledges, new wisdoms, and new possibilities. He or she will start to feel that this book actually makes sense to certain degrees. By then, he or she will slowly let in the light of awakening and would begin to embark on the journey of finding out his or her true self and his or her true existence here on Earth.

Changing perspectives is an important step in the journey of learning different dimensional cosmic lessons in the Known Universe and in the Goongverse. There are many new horizons awaiting in the higher dimensions for the third density entities to learn, to experience, and to explore. The third density entities on Earth should change their perspectives so they can change their lives. They should try their best to wake up and create the reality they have ever dreamed of while they are here on Earth. They should learn their third dimensional cosmic lessons so they can move up to the higher dimensions to learn and to experience so many exciting and marvelous things in the Known Universe, the Multiverse, the Megaverse, the Gigaverse, the Archverse and the Goongverse. They shouldn't keep themselves reincarnate here on Earth to play the same cosmic game over and over again for thousands of earth years without learning the cosmic lessons that they supposed to learn in order to graduate and move up to the higher dimensions.

Many cosmic workers might have known each other before volunteering on Earth, some might even volunteer on Earth as a group to accomplish a particular mission, however, when they came down to Earth, they got sucked into the dense third vibrational frequencies, they completely forget about their identities, their missions, and their volunteer fellows. At certain time in their lives on Earth, they would come into contact or interact with one another, but majority of the time they couldn't recognize each other. Sometimes one or two members of the volunteer group might be able to wake up and remember who they are while the other members of the group still deep asleep and have no idea about who they are and what they are here on Earth for. There's one cosmic volunteer group worth mentioning at this current spacetime, this cosmic volunteer group came to Earth to help with the betterment of the Earth and to help bring the third density entities on Earth to work together as one global nation to help speed up their cosmic learning process. There are five members in this volunteer group. Three members of this group are now holding great power on Earth. Each of them is a president of a powerful nation on Earth at this current spacetime. However, these three members of the group haven't been awakened. They still don't know that they are actually the cosmic workers who volunteered to come to Earth to help the third density entities with their cosmic lessons in this graduation cycle. Because they haven't been awakened yet, they still don't remember their true identities. Therefore, they fail to recognize each other and have completely forgotten about the mission they have signed up together before coming to Earth. Instead of trying to help the third density entities on Earth to work together so they can speed up their learning process, they actually try their best to protect the third density entities within their national borders only. Some members even issued many foreign policies to go against their cosmic volunteer fellows' countries. They fail to realize that they are actually from the same cosmic volunteer group who came to Earth to achieve the same mission. Of these three cosmic volunteer workers who are holding great power on Earth at this current spacetime, there's one cosmic volunteer worker has done many good things for the third density entities at the global level by offering a large number of the third density entities outside of his national borders to come to study and do research in his country for free. This entity hasn't initiated any wars with any countries up until this current spacetime. Hopefully he won't initiate any wars with any countries for the remaining of his volunteering time on Earth. One member of this volunteer group temporary got affected by the negative energy from the Anti Creator and has initiated war with his neighboring country in recent spacetime. Greed, fear, and the desire to have more power has opened up the door for the negative energy from the Anti Creator to penetrate in. One member of this group just got reelected the second time as the president of a powerful nation on Earth. These three cosmic volunteer workers have the power of preventing World War three from happening during the time they are holding great power on Earth. If they keep going against each other in their foreign policies, disagreeing in how to solve international conflicts, they can be the entities that would initiate World War three during the time they are holding great power on Earth. Hopefully they can recognize each other and start to work together to accomplish the mission they have signed up here on Earth. In order for them to recognize each other, they first need to wake up and remember who they are and what they are here on Earth for. The two remaining members of this volunteer group don't involve themselves in politics. They are in the process of awakening. They don't hold great power on Earth.

They both are working silently to help the third density entities on Earth at this current spacetime without knowing that they are actually members of a cosmic volunteer group and three members of their group are holding great power on Earth at this current spacetime.

Cosmic volunteer groups who volunteer to come to Earth at the same spacetime might not arrive on Earth at the same spacedate, some might arrive a few years earlier, some might arrive a few years later depending on the time they depart their higher dimension. Some entities might depart a few seconds or a few minutes earlier and end up arriving on Earth a few years earlier or a few decades earlier, some entities might depart a few seconds or a few minutes later and end up arriving on Earth a few years later or a few decades later because of the distortion of spacetime in different dimensions.

Many teachings on Earth at this current spacetime refer to the cosmic workers as starseeds. Actually, we are all starseeds. The ungraduated third density entities on Earth are starseeds as well since they all are not originated from Earth, they originated from every part of the Known Universe, the observable parts and the unobservable parts of the Known Universe. Due to the limitations of the knowledge about the origins of the third density entities on Earth and the limitations of the entities who gave out the knowledge, many teachings on Earth refer to the cosmic workers as starseeds and the rest of the third density entities on Earth aren't starseeds. While in reality, we are all starseeds after all. The iron in our blood is the same iron that giving out in any star explosions in the Known Universe. We all are starseeds. We all are the teeny tiny little stardusts that exist in the Known Universe at this current spacetime.

# Chapter 7

# The Cosmic Libraries

There are cosmic libraries in every verse within the Goongverse. In the universal verse, there are the universal libraries. Each individual Universe has its own library which cannot be accessed by any entities from other Universes. It can only be accessed by the entities within each individual Universe and the higher density entities from the Multiverse and the verses beyond where their host Universe is located within. Lower density entities cannot access the cosmic libraries from the higher dimensions. However, higher density entities can access all the cosmic libraries from the lower dimensions within their host Universe, host Multiverse, host Megaverse, host Gigaverse and host Archverse. Higher density entities in the goongversal verse can access all the cosmic libraries in all verses within the Goongverse.

In the Known Universe, the Universal Council keeps a record of all the ungraduated third density entities that got transported to Earth to learn their third dimensional cosmic lessons in the universal library. This record also records all the cosmic workers who have been volunteering on Earth to help the ungraduated third density entities on Earth. Some awakened cosmic workers and the third density entities with high vibrational frequencies can access this record. It is known to Earth as the Akashic record. The cosmic workers and the third density entities on Earth thought that the Akashic record is a compendium of all universal events, thoughts, words, emotions and intent ever to have occurred in the past, present, or future in terms of all entities and all lifeforms in all dimensions, not just the third density entities on Earth or those that volunteering on Earth. However, the record that the third density entities and the cosmic workers with high vibrational frequencies on Earth can access to is the record that only records all the events that related to all the third density entities that got transported to Earth and those cosmic workers who have been volunteering on Earth. There are many other records in the universal library in the Known Universe that held by the Universal Council. So far none of the cosmic workers or the third density entities on Earth have the abilities to access the other records because none of the cosmic workers or the third density entities have risen up their vibrational frequencies high enough in order to access the other records. They can only access the record that their vibrational frequencies are aligning with. Another reason why they can't access the other records besides the record that related to the third density entities and the cosmic workers on Earth is because the other records are irrelevant to the soul development processes of the third density entities on Earth. When the other records become relevant to their soul development processes or when they have moved up to the higher dimensions, they would be able to access them. Higher density entities such as the sixth and the seventh density entities with high vibrational frequencies can access the other records which record all the universal events that happened in the Known Universe to all entities from all dimensions in the Known Universe.

Since each individual Universe has its own universal library and it's inaccessible by any entities from any other Universes, this makes the entities from one Universe become completely unaware of the existences of the other entities from the other Universes. Only the seventh density entities from the highest sub-dimension of the seventh dimension who are ready to graduate and exit their host Universe and move up to the Multiverse where their host Universe is located can access all the universal libraries of other Universes which located within the Multiverse where they are about to move up to. They cannot access the universal libraries in other Universes which located in other Multiverses. Even the multiversal entities cannot access the universal libraries of other Universes which aren't located within their host Multiverse. The seventh density entities from the highest sub-dimension of the seventh dimension who aren't ready to graduate and exit the Known Universe yet don't have access to any cosmic libraries of any other Universes beside their host Universe.

In the multiversal verse, there are the multiversal libraries. Each Multiverse has its own library that cannot be accessed by any entities from the universal verse or any entities from other Multiverses. It can be accessed by the entities who have high vibrational frequencies within their host Multiverse. Higher density entities from the Megaverse can access all the multiversal libraries of the Multiverses which located within their host Megaverse. They cannot access the libraries of other Multiverses which aren't located within their host Megaverse. The eleventh density entities from the highest sub-dimension of the eleventh dimension who are ready to exit their host Multiverse and move up to the Megaverse where their host Multiverse is located can access all the multiversal libraries of each individual Multiverse within the Megaverse where they are about to graduate and move up to. They cannot access the multiversal libraries of other Multiverses which located in other Megaverses. Even the megaversal entities cannot access the multiversal libraries of other Multiverses which aren't located within their host Megaverse. Higher density entities beyond the megaversal verse can access all the multiversal libraries of the Multiverses which located within their host verse.

In the megaversal verse, there are the megaversal libraries. Each Megaverse has its own library which cannot be accessed by any entities below the megaversal verse and cannot be accessed by any entities from any other Megaverses. It can be accessed by the megaversal entities who have high vibrational frequencies within each individual Megaverse. Higher density entities from the Gigaverse can access all the megaversal libraries of the

Megaverses which located within their host Gigaverse. They cannot access the megaversal libraries of other Megaverses which aren't located within their host Gigaverse. The fifteenth density entities from the highest sub-dimension of the fifteenth dimension who are ready to exit their host Megaverse and move up to the Gigaverse where their host Megaverse is located can access all the megaversal libraries of the Megaverses which located within the Gigaverse where they are about to graduate and move up to. They cannot access the megaversal libraries of other Megaverses which located in other Gigaverses. Even the gigaversal entities cannot access the megaversal libraries of other Megaverses which aren't located within their host Gigaverse. Higher density entities beyond the gigaversal verse can access all the megaversal libraries of the Megaverses which located within their host verse.

In the gigaversal verse, there are the gigaversal libraries. Each Gigaverse has its own library which cannot be accessed by any entities below the gigaversal verse and cannot be accessed by any entities from any other Gigaverses. It can be accessed by the gigaversal entities who have high vibrational frequencies within their host Gigaverse. Higher density entities from the Archverse can access all the gigaversal libraries of the Gigaverses which located within their host Archverse. They cannot access the gigaversal libraries of other Gigaverses which aren't located within their host Archverse. The nineteenth density entities from the highest sub-dimension of the nineteenth dimension who are ready to graduate and exit their host Gigaverse and move up to the Archverse where their host Gigaverse is located can access all the gigaversal libraries of each individual Gigaverse which located within the Archverse where they are about to graduate and move up to. They cannot access the gigaversal libraries of other Gigaverses which located in other Archverses. Even the archversal entities cannot access the gigaversal libraries of other Gigaverses which aren't located within their host Archverse. Higher density entities beyond the archversal verse can access all the gigaversal libraries in the gigaversal verse.

In the archversal verse, there are the archversal libraries. Each Archverse has its own library which cannot be accessed by any lower density entities below the archversal verse and cannot be accessed by any entities from any other Archverses. It can be accessed by the archversal entities who have high vibrational frequencies within each individual Archverse. Higher density entities in the goongversal verse can access all the cosmic libraries in each individual Archverse. The entities from the goongversal verse also have the ability to access all the cosmic libraries from all the verses within the Goongverse. The archversal entities who are ready to graduate and move up to the Goongverse have the abilities to access all the archversal libraries of all Archverses. These entities also have the abilities to access all the cosmic libraries in the universal verse, the multiversal verse, the megaversal verse, and the gigaversal verse.

In the goongversal verse, there are the goongversal library. The goongversal library cannot be accessed by any lower density entities below the goongversal verse and cannot be accessed by any entities from any other parts of our cosmos. It can only be accessed by the goongversal entities who have high vibrational frequencies and the entities from the Creatorverse, the Godverse, and the Infinite Creatorverse.

# Chapter 8

# Extraterrestrials/Alien encounters

Extraterrestrial spaceships have been flying around Earth for eons, most of the time they don't want to show themselves up to the third density entities on Earth. In rare occasions, they might want to show themselves up to certain third density entities or certain cosmic workers if they see the situation is needed or suitable. The third density entities on Earth would never be able to see a spaceship from the higher dimensions if the entities from the higher dimensions don't want to show themselves to the third density entities.

However, for spaceships from other third density entities from other third dimensional planets in the Known Universe, it's easy for any third density entities on Earth to see. Earth has been visited many times by many spaceships from other third density entities from other planets. Many spaceships from Sirius star system have visited Earth. The third density entities from Sirius star system have very advanced and powerful technologies. The type of advanced and powerful technologies that once the ancestors of the third density entities on Earth were capable of developing before the Universal Council and the Galactic Council decided to do

103

the genetic alteration. Spaceships from other third density entities visiting Earth usually don't hide themselves from the third density entities on Earth. Any extraterrestrial spaceships that can be seen by the third density entities on Earth usually belong to other third density entities from other third dimensional planets in the Milky Way galaxy. Third density entities from other galaxies haven't visited Earth by spaceships yet.

Like the third density entities on Earth who are always curious about intelligent lifeforms from outer space, extraterrestrials from other third dimensional planets also very curious about intelligent lifeforms from outer space. They love to take samples of living lifeforms whenever they visit a new planet. Whenever they visited Earth, they always tried their best to take some samples of the third density entities on Earth. That's why many abductions have been reported. Depending on the species of extraterrestrials or how advanced their technologies or their spiritual awareness are, the abduction experiences can be different. Some extraterrestrials might give the third density entities on Earth a pleasant and warm feelings, while others might give the third density entities on Earth a scared and horrified feelings.

Besides the abductions from the third density entities from other planets, the negative polarized entities from the higher dimensions especially from the Orion Constellation also actively participate in the abductions. These negative entities are very selective with the third density entities that they want to abduct because they want to program these third density entities to use them for their benefits in the future. This type of abduction usually makes the third density entities on Earth feel restless and terrified. The experiences about the abductions aren't pleasant at all.

Cosmic workers on Earth who haven't been awakened once in a while also being contacted by aliens. The extraterrestrials that come to interact with the unawakened cosmic workers on Earth are the higher density entities who are in charge of monitoring the awakening process of the cosmic workers on Earth from the Galactic Council. The reason for this kind of interaction is to see which are the factors that have been keeping the cosmic workers fell deep asleep that they haven't been able to wake up. Members of the Galactic Council want to see if there's anything wrong with the programing with the cosmic workers. Even though the cosmic workers have to pass through the cosmic veil of forgetfulness in order to come to Earth and forget all about their identities from the higher dimensions, but they have been programmed to be awakened at certain point in their lives. Being abducted by the higher density entities such as members of the Galactic Council is a wonderful experience. Cosmic workers usually feel calm and pleasant as if they are in heaven or paradise. No anxiety or frustration occurs. Everything is so peaceful, magnificent and marvelous. Most of the time, members of the Galactic Council would wipe out memories of the cosmic workers about the interactions or encounters, but if the cosmic workers aware of the situation and ask the members of the Galactic Council to let them keep the memories and the experiences, the memories and the experiences about the extraterrestrial encounters wouldn't be wiped out. This kind of encounter usually done through beaming. The third density entity could be staying at home watching TV on a couch, the next milliseconds, they would find themselves inside a spaceship full of strange entities who are trying to examining them. Unawakened cosmic workers who are carrying important missions on Earth usually being contacted by members of the Galactic Council in this way. Awakened cosmic workers usually not being contacted by members of the Galactic Council in the same way. The reason why members of the Galactic Council don't try to contact the awakened cosmic workers physically because the awakened cosmic workers already be able to communicate telepathically with the entities from the higher dimensions and the entities from the Galactic Council.

Many spaceships from the third density entities from other third dimensional planets have been crashed on Earth in Earth's history. The authority groups on Earth knew about some of these crashes. There were certain collaborations between the authority groups on Earth and the third density entities from other planets. Many technologies on Earth at this current spacetime were given by the third density entities from other planets which have very advanced technologies. Many were also given by the negative polarized entities from the higher dimensions. The negative polarized entities from the higher dimensions want the third density entities on Earth to use the particular technologies that were given by them to cause destruction and chaos on Earth or to put the third density entities on Earth in control. Most of the time the authority groups on Earth would deny any extraterrestrial spaceship crashes or any collaborations between the third density entities on Earth with any third density entities from other planets in the Milky Way galaxy. There are many reasons that the authority groups on Earth don't want to expose this kind of information to the public. The first reason is that the authority groups don't want the public groups to panic. They think that the public groups aren't ready to accept this kind of information yet. The second reason is that Earth is being divided into many different countries and the authority group of each country would want to keep the extraterrestrial contacting secretly to themselves. They don't want to share it with any other countries.

Contacting or collaborating with other third density entities from other planets can help with scientific developments on Earth to certain degrees, however, since the spiritual awareness of the third density entities is relatively low throughout the Known Universe and in other Universes as well, the third density entities from other planets can be very aggressive and territorial seeking entities. They might be in search of expending territories outside of their host planet. The third density entities are the entities that can easily get affected by the negative energy from the Anti Creator, some third density entities from other planets that have advanced technologies might have the purpose of conquering other third dimensional planets instead of making peace. The third density entities on Earth should be very selective when it comes to contacting with other third density entities from other planets or collaborating or establishing relationship with them.

# Chapter 9

# Third Density Entity Lifecycle on Earth

Third density entity lifespan on Earth at this current spacetime is about 100 earth years. However, because of the unharmonious ways of living here on Earth, only a small percentage of the third density entities could reach up to the 100 earth years lifespan. In extremely rare cases, a few entities might live surpass the 100 earth years lifespan for a couple more years.

At the beginning of each lifecycle or each incarnation here on Earth, the third density entities would be able to remember their previous incarnation experiences. They would be able to carry on the memories of their previous incarnations up until when they reach the age of two. By then, the cosmic veil of forgetfulness completely penetrates in and they would forget all the memories of their past incarnation. If they could ever remember, it would be only a vague memory of it. This is the reason why the third density entities on Earth barely remember anything about their childhood since the day they were born up until the age of two. When they reach the age of two, the cosmic veil of forgetfulness completely penetrates in and wipes out the memories of their previous incarnation so they can start building memories of their current incarnation. They would be able to carry on all the memories of their current incarnation up until the age of two in their next incarnation on Earth. Newborns sometimes for no reason would laugh or smile to themselves. This is because they are actually living in the memories of their previous incarnation at that moment. For the third density entities who have made it to the graduation and no longer have to reincarnate back to Earth to learn their third dimensional cosmic lessons, they would be able to carry all the memories of all their incarnations here on Earth up to the higher dimensions.

When the third density entities at the last couple minutes of their lives here on Earth, their brains usually work excessively to collect all the memories they have built in their current incarnation to carry up to the lower astral plane where they would wait for their next incarnation. For those entities who have made it to the graduation, they can either wait in the lower astral plane for the graduation period to approach so the portals would be opened for them to move up to the higher dimensions where they would learn their next level of cosmic lessons or they can choose to reincarnate back to Earth again to help other third density entities as cosmic workers. The process of collecting memories right before leaving their physical bodies on Earth of the third density entities can be monitored and detected by the current technologies on Earth. Scientists can monitor the activities of the third density entities' brains right before they leave their physical bodies to see that their brains actually work excessively to collect all the memories right before they leave their physical bodies on Earth.

The process of leaving the physical bodies when it comes to an end of each incarnation actually is not painful or scary for the entities who are undergoing through the process. Couple of minutes before they leave their physical bodies, the third density entities no longer be able to feel any pains or discomforts in their physical bodies. They don't even know that they are about to leave their physical bodies. All of a sudden, they find themselves in a place that surrounded by many wonderful things or they find themselves in the middle of a life event that they have always been dreaming of. The dreamed life that they have always been dreaming of suddenly appears. The event in the dreamed life will lead them into the invisible world. Near the very end of the process, the dreamed life becomes so vivid, so clear and so real that the life in the physical world no longer feels real to them. They will start to follow the event in the dreamed life and moving deeper and deeper into the invisible world. Life in the physical world completely no longer feels real to them. They keep on sinking deeper and deeper into the dreamed life in the invisible world until they completely leave behind their physical bodies. Leaving the physical bodies behind is actually the process of living the dreamed life that the third density entities on Earth have ever dreamed of in a very short period of time. The third density entities that going through

111

the process are actually at the happiest moment of their lives in their whole incarnation on Earth.

The third density entities who are observing the process of other third density entities leaving their physical bodies behind are the entities that aware of the process. They know that the other third density entities are in the process of leaving their physical bodies behind. They usually would be in shocked or in pain especially if the third density entities who are in the process of leaving their physical bodies behind are their love ones. Observing the love ones in the process of leaving their physical bodies behind is the type of pain that no words on Earth could ever express it or describe it. Observing the love ones leaving behind their bodies in the physical world and move into the invisible world is the most painful thing that any third density entities on Earth could have ever experienced. Hopefully, after knowing that at the moment the third density entities leaving their physical bodies behind in the physical world is the moment that the third density entities are at the happiest stage of their life in their whole incarnation, maybe it would help ease the pains of the third density entities who are observing the process and staying behind in the physical world after their love ones have finished one of their incarnations on Earth.

The thing that the third density entities on Earth afraid of the most is that one day they have to leave Earth. They have to leave behind everything they have ever built in their whole incarnation and they have to leave behind their love ones. No one would ever feel ready for it. No one would ever want to leave Earth because they don't know what will happen to them after they leave. Would it be the end of their whole existence in the Cosmos or the beginning of something new that they aren't ready to experience. They are afraid of the unknown world beyond Earth. Whether the third density entities on Earth want it or not, everyone must leave Earth when it come to an end of each incarnation. For the entities who couldn't make it to the graduation, leaving Earth is only temporary. They will be sent back to Earth again for them to relearn their third dimensional cosmic lessons in different third dimensional physical bodies. This kind of leaving is to clear out whatever mindsets or whatever obstacles that preventing the third density entities from learning the third dimensional cosmic lessons in the current incarnation. When they got sent back, they would come back to Earth with a brand-new mindset and an empty brain that are ready to learn and absorb any cosmic lessons which being offered by the third dimensional cosmic school. It's always easier to teach a young entity who knows nothing than teaching an old entity who thinks he or she already knows everything. A young entity is always eager to learn and ready to open his or her mind to learn anything new. An old entity usually no longer wants to open his or her mind to learn anything new or to believe in anything different from what he or she already knew or believed. Leaving Earth temporarily is only a tiny reset for the third density entities on Earth to have a higher chance of learning their third dimensional cosmic lessons. It's only the end of one of their many incarnations where they couldn't learn their third dimensional cosmic lessons in order to move up to the fourth dimension. It's the beginning of their new learning journey, a new starting over for them to relearn their third dimensional cosmic lessons so they can move up to the fourth dimension and higher.

For the third entities who have learned all of their third dimensional cosmic lessons and are ready to move up to the fourth dimension or higher, leaving Earth when it comes to an end of their incarnation can be permanent or temporary. For the third density entities who already made it to the graduation, if they no longer want to come back to Earth to help the other third density entities, leaving Earth would be permanent for them. They would move up to the fourth dimension where they will learn their fourth dimensional cosmic lessons to prepare themself to graduate and move up to the fifth dimension. For the third density entities who already made it to the graduation and move up to the fourth dimension but still wanting to come back to help the other third density entities, leaving Earth after the end of their incarnation would be only temporary. They can come back to Earth again as cosmic workers to help the third density entities on Earth.

For the cosmic workers, when they have finished their cosmic missions on Earth, they can leave Earth permanently or temporarily. They can go back to the higher dimensions where they originally came from and never volunteer back to Earth again or they can volunteer to come back to Earth again to help the third density entities with their third dimensional cosmic lessons.

One thing worth mentioning in the third density entity lifecycle on Earth is sleeping. The third density entities spend one-third of their time on Earth sleeping. This means that if a third density entity lives up to the age of 100, he or she would spend 33.3 years of his or her life here on Earth sleeping. Sleeping not only allows their physical bodies to repair and regenerate, but it also allows their souls (the essence of their true selves) to travel out of their physical bodies to explore the world beyond the physical plane. Sleeping also helps cosmic workers get messages or guidance from the higher dimensions. Many instructions or messages from the higher dimensions usually given to the third density entities or cosmic workers on Earth through their dreams. Cosmic workers who have their twin souls volunteering on other planets can meet each other in their dreams whether they could recognize each other in their dreams or not. Entities with high vibrational frequencies can travel to different dimensions in the Known Universe through their dreams. It's dreaming, but it's actually not a dream, it's the reality in other dimensions that appears in the form of dreams to the third density entities or cosmic workers here on Earth.

# Chapter 10

# The Cosmic Creator School

The Goongverse was created as a cosmic creator school for training and building future cosmic creators. The idea started out with the Infinite Creator in the Infinite Godverse. The Infinite Creator is the one and the only Ruler of our vast Cosmos. Below the Infinite Creator are the Gods and Deities. The Gods and Deities are the entities who are assisting the Infinite Creator with the management of our Cosmos. The Gods and Deities are the entities that reside in the Godverse. As the Cosmos continues to expand, the Infinite Creator wants to have more and more celestial objects and celestial lifeforms that are far more diverse, far more exceptional, far more fascinating, and far more entertaining that he couldn't think of creating to exist in our Cosmos. He gave the idea to the God Council in the Godverse. After carefully considering, the God Council decided to give the mission to one powerful entity in the Cosmos. The Thought entity. The Thought entity is the entity who has the power to manifest or create anything with only one thought. He can control, manage, and manipulate a great amount of matter, energy, particle and almost everything that exists in the Cosmos if he has the permission to do so from the God Council or the

Infinite Creator. He is ranking as the fourth most powerful entity in the Cosmos right after the Deities, the Gods, and the Infinite Creator. Since the day he was created, the Thought entity was just floating around in every part of the Cosmos without actually creating anything. He was still inactive. When he was called upon to carry out the mission by the God Council, he came to realize the creator power he has within him. His cosmic creator power got activated. The Thought entity spent a great amount of time thinking of what he could create that would impress the God Council and the Infinite Creator, he came across the idea of creating many creators which have the same ability of creating like him so that they can create plentiful of new and unthinkable celestial objects or celestial lifeforms that he alone couldn't think of creating. These entities must go through strict cosmic trainings before they can qualify themselves as cosmic creators. Unlike the Thought entities which was created by the Infinite Creator, since the day he was created, everything was already infused into him by the Infinite Creator, he didn't go through any cosmic trainings in order to become a cosmic creator in the Creatorverse. Because he didn't go through any cosmic trainings, sometimes he might not be able to control his creator instinct and might create excessively. That's why the Infinite Creator even created one entity to keep the Thought entity in check in case the Thought entity might be over-creating. That entity was created at the same time the Thought entity was created.

The Thought entity wants all the future cosmic creators be the disciplined cosmic creators and be able to control and balance out between their desire to create and the equilibrium of their surroundings, that's why all the future cosmic creators must go through strict cosmic trainings. The Thought Entity gave the idea to the God Council; the God Council thought it was a brilliant idea. The Thought entity immediately started to create the cosmic school for building future cosmic creators, the Goongverse. He was very eager about it and nonstop creating day and night. In no time, the Goongverse was created. He was officially known as the Creator of the Goongverse in our Cosmos.

There are twenty-seven dimensions in the Goongverse and each dimension offers unique cosmic lessons for the development processes of all the entities residing in it. All the entities in the Goongverse have to start their lessons from the first dimension and learn their ways up to the twenty-seventh dimension. When the cosmic lessons in all twenty-seven dimensions in the Goongverse have been learned, they would be able to graduate from the Goongverse and move up to the Creatorverse to become the true cosmic creators.

The Goongverse is the cosmic creator school for building and creating future cosmic creators. This is the place in the Cosmos that giving birth to new cosmic creators and nourishing them from the first dimension up to the twenty-seventh dimension where they would graduate from the creator school and become the true cosmic creators in the

Creatorverse. Once they enter the Creatorverse, they would be at the same level as the Creator of the Goongverse. Because of all the cosmic trainings and cosmic soul lessons they have learned in the twenty-seven dimensions in the Goongverse, they would be able to create many new verses, new celestial objects, and new celestial lifeforms that are far more diverse and far more superior than the current Goongverse. The purpose of the imperfections in the Goongverse is to create a perfect environment for building and creating the most perfect and the most resilient future cosmic creators. Imperfections are always catalysts for building perfections in the Cosmos.

All the cosmic soul lessons in different dimensions in the Goongverse are for building kindness, compassion, love, selflessness, resilience, empathy, confidence, accountability, humility, adaptability, positivity, integrity, flexibility, harmony, tolerance, etc. in the future cosmic creators. Since the Creator of the Goongverse already infused his creator instinct into all the entities in the Goongverse, as the entities in the Goongverse graduate from one dimension and move up to another dimension, or from one verse and move up to another verse, they automatically unlock their creator power according to the dimension or the verse that they are graduating and moving up to. In every dimension, there are matter, particle, energy, and everything that are needed for them to exercise and practice their creator power. It's the soul lessons that the Creator of the Goongverse couldn't infuse into them, they must learn and experience the soul

119

lessons personally in every dimension by themselves in order for them to grow into strong, harmonious, and resilient future cosmic creators. In every dimension, they must learn to balance out their creator power with their soul development processes. If they focus too much on their creator power, they might develop some advanced technologies that could end up wiping themselves out before they could learn their cosmic lessons for their soul development purposes. If destruction occurs, they would have to restart learning their cosmic lessons again in that particular dimension. It would be so much harder for them to relearn their cosmic lessons after each destruction because it takes time for their souls to heal from the cosmic traumas they had experienced before they can start focusing on learning their cosmic soul lessons again.

When the Goongverse had been created and all the cosmic lessons in every dimension and every verse had been set. Many entities in the Goongverse had learned their first and second dimensional cosmic lessons and moved up to the third dimension to learn their third dimensional cosmic lessons, then came an intruder, he is an entity who has almost the same level of cosmic power as the Creator of the Goongverse. His cosmic power is only slightly below the cosmic power of the Creator of the Goongverse. This entity is the opposite of the Creator of the Goongverse. He was created at the same time the Creator of the Goongverse was created. He is the entity that the Infinite Creator created to keep the Thought entity in check in case the Thought entity

Moving to the Unseen World

might be over-creating. He is the negative Thought entity. Just like the Creator of the Goongverse, the negative Thought entity was inactive since the day he was created. When he came across the Goongverse and saw what the Creator of the Goongverse had created, he got interested in the project. The idea of wanting to interfere kept growing stronger and stronger within him. Finally, he couldn't resist the temptation and started to interfere. His cosmic power got activated. He decided to build a verse orbiting around the Goongverse, the Anti Creatorverse. He has been residing in the Anti Creatorverse since then. He has been constantly infusing negative energy into the Goongverse to interfere with the soul development processes of all the entities in every verse and every dimension in the Goongverse. Since he was created as the opposite of the Creator of the Goongverse, whatever the Creator of the Goongverse does, he would do the opposite. The Creator of the Goongverse was created to build and to create while he was created to demolish and to destroy. The Creator of the Goongverse saw the seriousness of the matter, he immediately created a verse orbiting around the Goongverse, the Protectorverse, and has been residing in this verse since then. The Creator of the Goongverse has been constantly infusing positive energy into the Goongverse to neutralize the negative energy from the Anti Creator. He immediately sealed all the portals between the verses in the Goongversal hierarchy to stop the entities that got affected by the negative energy from going through. Only the entities who don't get affected by the negative energy from the Anti Creator or the entities that could remove all the negative energy after being affected and polarize positively again can go through the portals between the verses once they have learned all of their cosmic lessons in that particular verse in the Goongversal hierarchy. The entities that got affected by the negative energy from the Anti Creator and polarize negatively can move between dimensions within the same verse when they finish learning their selfish and destructive lessons that set by the Anti Creator, but they cannot move from one verse to another verse. The highest dimension they can move up to in the same verse is the highest sub-dimension of the dimension right below the highest dimension in their host Verse. When they reach the highest sub-dimension of the dimension below the highest dimension in their host verse, they would automatically be reset and get pushed down to the dimension where they first started to polarize negatively for them to relearn their cosmic lessons. If they still polarize negatively, they would have to repeat the process over and over again until they turn to polarize positively and learn all the cosmic lessons in that particular verse where they are residing in, then they can graduate and move up to another verve to learn their next cosmic lessons in the Goongversal hierarchy.

The God Council saw the interference of the Anti Creator as a perfect catalyst for building exceptional resilient future cosmic creators. The entities that could make it to the graduation and exit the Goongverse under the influence of the negative energy from the Anti Creator would carry all the exceptional qualities that they are looking for in a cosmic creator. The God Council let the Anti Creator continue to do whatever he was doing. Even though his intention wasn't pure, but the God Council and the Creator of the Goongverse could use it to benefit the trainings of the future cosmic creators.

All entities in the Goongverse were created with the ability to build because they all have the creator instinct within them. What they weren't being created with are the cosmic soul lessons that they must learn in the twenty-seven dimensions in the Goongverse. Since the cosmic soul lessons couldn't be infused into them by the Creator of the Goongverse, they must learn and experience all the cosmic soul lessons by themselves. They must be able to balance between their soul development processes and their creator power in every dimension and every verse. When their creator power exceeds their soul development processes, destructions always occur.

The cosmic school for building the future cosmic creators in the Goongverse seems very complex with so many cosmic lessons needed to be learned in such a lengthy period of time that the third density entities on Earth couldn't even imagine. To make it easier and simpler for the third density entities on Earth to understand, just imagine that the first three density entities in the universal verse are like the preschoolers, the fourth density entities up to the seventh density entities in the universal verse are like the primary schoolers, the multiversal entities are like the middle schoolers, the

123

megaversal entities are like the high schoolers, the gigaversal entities are like the four years university students, the archversal entities are like the master students, and the Goongversal entities are like the PhD students. The difference between the cosmic creator school and the schools which created by the third density entities on Earth is that the cosmic creator school offers real life experiences through each and every lesson in every dimension while the schools which created by the third density entities on Earth mainly offering theoretical experiences, students who graduated from the schools which created by the third density on Earth have to learn the real life experiences after they have graduated from the theoretical schools, which makes the schools that built by the third density entities on Earth very impractical.

## 10.1 The Universal Creator Students

All entities in the Goongverse were created with the abilities to build and to create. The Creator of the Goongverse infused his creator instinct into each and every individual entity in the Goongverse. Starting from the second dimension in the universal verse, the creator instinct already clearly appears in each individual entity. The second density entities already have strong desire to build and to create. They already start to build and create their own societies. For example, the second density entities such as ants already have strong instinct to build. Not only they know how to build home or shelters, but they also know how to build a complex society. Ant colonies have a highly complex social structure. Within each ant colony, there is a hierarchy of roles and responsibilities that helps the colony function as a whole. The workers are responsible for gathering food and caring for the young. The soldiers are responsible for protecting the colony from predators and other threats. The reproductives (the queen and drones) are responsible for producing new members of the colony. With strong survival instinct and strong creator instinct, ants already be able to build a society with complex hierarchy that is essential for the survival of their colony.

The third density entities are fearless little creators, fearless little builders in the universal verse. Not only they can build houses and shelters, they also can build roads, vehicles, aircrafts, or anything that are needed for their survival or for their pleasure or for making their lives easier in the third dimension. They also can build satellites or tiny satellite planets that orbiting around their host planets. They can build society with a hierarchy almost as complex as the goongversal hierarchy but in a much smaller scale. They even try to manipulate and control the weather, build equipment that can harness the energy from the Sun, and collaborate with other third density entities from other third dimensional planets to build spaceships that can travel at the speed of light or can travel through space portals. (These are the third density entities from other planets, the third density entities on Earth at this current spacetime not yet capable of building spaceships that can travel at the speed of light or travel through space portals).

The third density entities are the little genetic masters in the physical plane. Not only they can alter the genes of many second density entities, they also try to experiment with the genetic alteration of their own species. It might be hard for some third density entities on Earth to believe that the Universal Council and the Galactic Council actually did the genetic alteration to the third density entities on Earth, if any entities feel it's hard to believe, he or she should look at what the third density entities on Earth capable of doing, with very little genetic knowledge, the third density entities on Earth already capable of altering the genes of the second density entities and the third density entities. Therefore, it's not that hard to believe that the Universal Council and the Galactic Council actually did the genetic alteration 5 times to the third density entities on Earth.

The third density entities are ambitious little creators, sometimes they even build or create objects that are far beyond their ability to control. Many times, in the history of the Known Universe, the third density entities had developed advanced technologies that ended up destroying themselves and their own civilizations. It's the same in Earth's history, many third density entities had developed advanced technologies that ended up destroying their own civilizations. The most recent civilization that ended up destroying themself due to their advanced technologies was the Atlantis.

At this current spacetime, the third density entities on Earth are again about to repeat the history of their ancestors with the development of artificial intelligence that they can't fully control. The main cosmic lessons for the third density entities on Earth to learn are the lessons of love and compassion. Artificial intelligence that the third density entities on Earth trying to create at this current spacetime are not capable of understanding what love or compassion is, they wouldn't even hesitate for a second to terminate the lives of any third density entities on Earth if they think those third density entities are interfering or standing in their ways. This current spacetime is very crucial for the third density entities on Earth since Earth is in the duration of the third graduation period. Earth has entered the graduation period since 2021. The duration of each graduation period is about 50 earth years which means that the duration of the graduation will end in the year of 2071 on Earth. If the third density entities cannot make it to the graduation in this graduation cycle, they would have to wait another 75 thousand earth years for the next graduation cycle to take place. The Universal Council, the Galactic Council, and many higher density entities are watching this graduation cycle closely with the hope that many third density entities on Earth would be able to make it to the graduation without putting themselves in the path of destruction like their ancestors did due to advanced development of technologies on Earth at this current spacetime.

Technology developments in any dimension or any verse in the Goongversal hierarchy should be in harmonious and aligned with the spiritual developments or spiritual awareness. When technology developments surpass spiritual awareness, destructions always occur. When destructions occur, the cosmic entities that have been through the destructions always carry so much cosmic trauma that it would take a long time for them to heal before they can start focusing on learning their cosmic soul lessons in the same dimension again. One vivid example for this is the destruction of planet Kong in the Solar System which blew the planet into pieces and turned it to become the asteroid belt between Mars and Jupiter. Some third density entities on planet Kong got transported to Earth through soul transport after their planet got blew up are still struggling with their cosmic trauma at this current spacetime on Earth. So much time has passed and so many incarnations they have been through on Earth, but they still couldn't completely get out of the cosmic trauma that they had experienced from their previous home planet in order to focus on learning their third dimensional cosmic lessons again.

All living entities in the Goongverse are the cosmic creator students. They are constantly nonstop creating. No matter which dimension or which verse they are residing in, they constantly create new objects or new lifeforms with whatever particle or material that they have access to or with whatever matter, particle, or energy from space that they can control and manipulate. Lower density entities can create celestial objects, lifeform, and societies that are far less complex and in a much smaller scale. Higher density entities can create celestial objects, lifeforms, and societies that are far more complex, sophisticated, and in a much larger scale. Every day, there are new celestial objects and new celestial lifeforms being created in the Goongverse. Genetic alterations are happening every day in every verse and every dimension. Each time when a genetic alteration occurs, a new species of lifeforms is being created and being added to the celestial lifeforms in the Goongverse.

The fourth density entities are the planetary creators. They have the ability to create and manage a planet and its moons such as the Earth and its moon or Saturn and its moons. They can build objects that can harness energy from the star system or the nearby star systems to use for their daily lives. To the third density entities on Earth or on any other third dimensional planets, whatever the fourth density entities and the higher density entities can build or create, they all seem as if the Creator of the Creatorverse, the Gods, or the Infinite Creator have built or created them. The third density entities on Earth have the tendency of thinking that whoever are above them or more powerful than them must be the Gods, the Creator of the Goongverse or the Infinite Creator.

The fifth density entities are the star system creators. They have the ability to build and create a star system like the Solar System or the Alpha Centauri System, etc. They can arrange and rearrange the orbits of each planet in the star system to make sure their orbits don't interfere or collide with one another within the star system. The fifth density entities are highly intellectual entities in the universal verse. The fifth dimension is the wisdom hub of each individual Universe in the universal verse since most entities in the fifth dimension usually spend more time gaining knowledge about their host Universe rather than spending time building or creating. They still build and create since they all have the creator instinct within them, but the time they spend to build or create is much lesser than the time they spend on gaining more wisdom and knowledge about their host Universe. The fifth density entities have the ability to merge two or more planets in the lower dimensions together to create a giant planet. The sixth density entities usually aid the fifth density entities with the building or creating of a new star system or merging of two planets in the lower dimensions.

The sixth density entities are the galactic creators. They can build and create galaxies like the Milky Way galaxy or the Andromeda galaxy, etc. They are also the creators of dwarf galaxies. The sixth density entities are powerful creators in the universal verse. They are the entities who can decide whether or not to merge one planet with another or one star system with another to create a larger planet or a larger star system to serve the soul development purposes of the lower density entities below the sixth dimension. Because they are powerful creators, they must learn how to balance between their creator power and their spiritual awareness. Any misbalances or misuses in their creator power can cause massive destruction at the galactic level within their host Universe.

The seventh density entities are the creators of clusters of galaxies, superclusters of galaxies, supercluster galaxies systems such as the BOSS Great Wall, and everything within their host Universe. They are the entities that keep their host Universe functioning properly without collapsing. They are the most powerful creators in the universal verse. The third density entities on Earth mainly think of them as the Infinite Creator, the Gods or the Creator of the Goongverse since they are directly involved in the development processes of the third density entities on Earth in the physical plane. Additionally, the third density entities on Earth don't have access to any knowledge beyond the Known Universe. All the cosmic workers volunteered on Earth in the past came from the fourth dimension up to the sixth dimension. They don't have access to the knowledge beyond the Known Universe; therefore, they thought that the seventh dimension is the highest dimension in our Cosmos. They passed down this knowledge to the third density entities on Earth. That's why many third density entities on Earth actually think that the seventh dimension is the highest dimension in the Cosmos and the seventh density entities are the Creator of the Goongverse, the Gods, or the Infinite Creator. To the third density entities on Earth, the power that the seventh density entities possess is far beyond their imagination. The seventh density entities can alter or change how things operate in each individual Universe. The seventh density entities who are members of the Universal Council can decide when to merge two or more galaxies together to create one massive galaxy. They can decide whether or not to change the genetic structure of the lower density entities in the universal verse when they see it's appropriate for the soul development processes of the lower density entities at a particular spacetime. They are like the Gods or the Creators who are in charge of what is going on within their host Universe. They are the entities that directly involve with the soul development processes of entities in all seven dimensions. Therefore, the third density entities classify them as the Gods or the Infinite Creator of their host Universe is actually understandable and appropriate.

## 10.2 The Multiversal Creator Students

Eighth density entities, ninth density entities, tenth density entities, and eleventh density entities are the entities that reside in each individual Multiverse in the multiversal verse. The eighth density entities are the lowest density entities in each individual Multiverse. The eighth density entities are the creators of each individual Universe and its Dwarf Universes. The eighth density entities are the entities in charge of assisting the soul development processes of the seventh density entities in the universal verse. To the seventh density entities in the universal verse, the eighth density entities are godlike to them. When the eighth density entities offer their volunteer services to the universal verse, they only offer services to the seventh density entities who are in the highest sub-dimension of the seventh dimension. They can't offer their services to the sixth density entities or lower because the sixth density entities or lower cannot connect with the eighth density entities due to their low vibrational frequencies. The eighth density entities only offer services to the seventh density entities telepathically. They don't offer services physically in the universal verse after they have exited the universal verse and moved up to the multiversal verse.

The ninth density entities are the creators of clusters of universes. Each cluster of universes consists of thousands to several hundred thousand Universes and their Dwarf Universes. The ninth density entities are the entities that have the ability to merge two or more Universes together to create one massive Universe to serve the soul development purposes of the entities in the universal verse. The ninth density entities also assist the eighth density entities with the creation of each individual Universe in the universal verse.

The tenth density entities are the creators of supercluster systems of universes. Each supercluster system of universes contains a massive collection of universe clusters and universe groups that being held together by the gravitational force that the tenth density entities emitting out. The tenth density entities are the entities that have the ability to merge two or more clusters of universes together to create one massive cluster of universes.

The eleventh density entities are the creators of everything within their host Multiverse. They are the highest entities in the multiversal verse. They are the entities that hold their host Multiverse together and keep it functioning properly without collapsing. They are also the entities that oversee all the soul development processes of all the entities within their host Multiverse. They are the entities that have the ability to merge two or more supercluster systems of universes together to create one massive supercluster system of universes when they see it's appropriate for the soul development purposes of the entities below the eleventh dimension at a particular spacetime. The eleventh density entities are godlike to the lower density entities within their host Multiverse.

## 10.3 The Megaversal Creator Students

Twelfth density entities, thirteenth density entities, fourteenth density entities and fifteenth density entities are the entities that reside in each individual Megaverse in the megaversal verse. The twelfth density entities are the creators of each individual Multiverse and its Dwarf Multiverses. The Twelfth density entities are the entities that in charge of overseeing the soul development processes of the eleventh density entities in the multiversal verse and assisting them with their graduation from the multiversal verse to the megaversal verse. The Twelfth density entities offer assistant services to the eleventh density entities in the multiversal verse telepathically. Only the eleventh density entities who are in the highest sub-dimension of the eleventh dimension can access their services. Entities from the tenth dimension and below cannot access the services which offered by the twelfth density entities because of their low vibrational frequencies.

The thirteenth density entities are the creators of clusters of multiverses. Each cluster of multiverses consists of thousands to several hundred thousand Multiverses. The thirteenth density entities are the entities that have the ability to merge two or more Multiverses together to create one massive Multiverse to serve the soul development purposes of the lower density entities at a particular spacetime. The thirteenth density entities are the entities that assist the twelfth density entities with the creation of each individual Multiverse in the multiversal verse.

The fourteenth density entities are the creators of supercluster systems of multiverses. Each supercluster system of multiverses consists of massive collection of multiverse clusters. The fourteenth density entities are the entities that have the ability to merge two or more clusters of multiverses together to create a massive cluster of multiverses.

The fifteenth density entities are the creators of everything within their individual Megaverse. They are the highest entities in the megaversal verse. They are the entities that hold their host Megaverse together and keep it functioning properly without collapsing. They are also the entities that oversee all the soul development processes of all the entities within their host Megaverse. They are the entities that have the ability to merge two or more supercluster systems of multiverses together to create one massive supercluster system of multiverses when they see it's appropriate for the soul development purposes of the multiversal entities at a particular spacetime. The fifteenth density entities are godlike to the lower density entities within their host Megaverse.

## 10.4 The Gigaversal Creator students

Sixteenth density entities, seventeenth density entities, eighteenth density entities, and nineteenth density entities are the entities residing in each individual Gigaverse in the gigaversal verse. The sixteenth density entities are the creators of each individual Megaverse and its Dwarf Megaverses. The sixteenth density entities are the entities that in charge of overseeing the soul development processes of the fifteenth density entities in the megaversal verse and assisting them with their graduation from their host Megaverse to the Gigaverse where their host Megaverse is located. The sixteenth density entities offer assistant services to the fifteenth density entities in the megaversal verse telepathically. Only the fifteenth density entities who are in the highest sub-dimension of the fifteenth dimension in the megaversal verse can access the assistance of the sixteenth density entities from the gigaversal verse. The fourteenth density entities and below in the Megaversal verse can't access the services which offered by the sixteenth density entities telepathically because of their low vibrational frequencies.

The seventeenth density entities are the creators of clusters of megaverses. Each cluster of megaverses consists of thousands to several hundred thousand Megaverses. The seventeenth density entities are the entities that have the ability to merge two or more Megaverses together to create one massive Megaverse to serve the soul development purposes of the entities residing in the megaversal verse at a particular spacetime when they see it's necessary. The seventeenth density entities are the entities that assisting the sixteenth density entities with the creation of each individual Megaverse in the megaversal verse.

The eighteenth density entities are the creators of supercluster systems of megaverses. Each supercluster system of megaverses consists of massive collection of megaverse clusters. The eighteenth density entities are the entities that have the ability to merge two or more clusters of megaverses together to create one massive cluster of megaverses.

The nineteenth density entities are the creators of everything within their host Gigaverse. They are the highest entities in the gigaversal verse. They are the entities that hold their individual Gigaverse together and keep it functioning properly without collapsing. They are also the entities that oversee all the soul development processes of all the entities within their host Gigaverse. They are the entities that have the ability to merge two or more supercluster systems of megaverses together to create one massive supercluster system of megaverses when they see it's appropriate for the soul development processes of the megaversal entities at a particular spacetime. The nineteenth density entities are godlike to the lower density entities within their host Gigaverse.

## 10.5 The Archversal Creator Students

Twentieth density entities, twenty-first density entities, twenty-second density entities, and twenty-third density entities are the entities residing in each individual Archverse in the archversal verse. The twentieth density entities are the creators of each individual Gigaverse and its Dwarf Gigaverses which orbiting around each individual Gigaverse. The twentieth density entities are the entities that in charge of overseeing the soul development processes of the nineteenth density entities in the gigaversal verse and assisting them with the graduation process from the gigaversal verse to the archversal verse. The twentieth density entities offer assistant services to the nineteenth density entities in the gigaversal verse telepathically. Only the nineteenth density entities who are in the highest sub-dimension of the nineteenth dimension in the gigaversal verse can access the assistance of the twentieth density entities from the archversal verse. The eighteenth density entities and below in the gigaversal verse cannot access the volunteer services which offered by the twentieth density entities telepathically because of their low vibrational frequencies.

The twenty-first density entities are the creators of clusters of gigaverses. Each cluster of gigaverses consists of thousands to several hundred thousand Gigaverses. The twenty-first density entities are the entities that have the ability to merge two or more Gigaverses together to create one massive Gigaverse to serve the soul development purposes of the gigaversal entities at a particular spacetime when they see it's necessary. The twenty-first density entities are the entities that assist the twentieth density entities with the creation of each Gigaverse in the gigaversal verse.

The twenty-second density entities are the creators of supercluster systems of gigaverses. Each supercluster system of gigaverses consists of massive collection of gigaverse clusters. The twenty-second density entities are the entities that have the ability to merge two or more clusters of gigaverses together to create one massive cluster of gigaverses.

The twenty-third density entities are the creators of everything within their host individual Archverse. They are the highest entities in the archversal verse. They are the entities that hold their host Archverse together and keep it functioning properly without collapsing. They are also the entities that oversee all the soul development processes of all the entities within their host Archverse. They are the entities that have the ability to merge two or more supercluster systems of gigaverses together to create one massive supercluster system of gigaverses when they see it's appropriate for the soul development purposes of the lower density entities at a particular spacetime. The twenty-third density entities are godlike to the lower density entities within their host Archverse.

## 10.6 The Goongversal Creator Students

Twenty-fourth density entities, twenty-fifth density entities, twenty-sixth density entities, and twenty-seventh density entities are the entities residing in the highest goongversal hierarchy in the goongversal verse. The twenty-fourth density entities are the creators of each individual Archverse and its Dwarf Archverses which orbiting around each individual Archverse. The twenty-fourth density entities are the entities that are in charge of overseeing the soul development processes of the twenty-third density entities in the archversal verse and assisting them with the graduation process from the archversal verse to the goongversal verse. The twenty-fourth density entities offer assistant services to the twenty-third density entities in each Archverse telepathically. Only the twenty-third density entities who are in the highest sub-dimension of the twenty-third dimension in the archversal verse can access the assistance of the twenty-fourth density entities from the goongversal verse. The twenty-second density entities and lower in the archversal verse cannot access the volunteer services which offered by the twenty-fourth density entities telepathically because of their low vibrational frequencies.

The twenty-fifth density entities are the creators of clusters of archverses. Each cluster of archverses consists of thousands to several hundred thousand Archverses. The twenty-fifth density entities are the entities that have the ability to merge two or more Archverses together to create one massive Archverse to serve the soul development purposes of the entities residing in the archversal verse at a particular spacetime when they see it's necessary.

The twenty-sixth density entities are the creators of supercluster systems of archverses. Each supercluster system of archverses consists of massive collection of archverse clusters. The twenty-sixth density entities are the entities that have the ability to merge two or more clusters of archverses together to create one massive cluster of archverses to serve the soul development purposes of the entities residing in those clusters of archverses at a particular spacetime when they see it's necessary.

The twenty-seventh density entities are the creators of everything within the Goongverse. They are the highest entities in the Goongverse. They are the entities that keep everything in the Goongverse functioning properly without collapsing. They are also the entities that oversee all the soul development processes of all the entities in the Goongverse. They are the entities that have the ability to merge two or more supercluster systems of archverses together to create one massive supercluster system of archverses when they see it's appropriate for the soul development purposes of the lower density entities at a particular spacetime. The twenty-seventh density entities are the entities that would be considered as Gods, or the Creator of the Goongverse, or the Infinite Creator to the lower density entities in the entire Goongverse.

The third density entities in the universal verse don't know the existence of any entities beyond the universal verse. Only the seventh density entities in the highest sub-dimension of the seventh dimension who are ready to graduate and exit their host Universe have access to the knowledge of the eighth dimension in the Multiverse where they are about to move up to. Any entities exist beyond the eighth dimension are unknown to the ready to graduate seventh density entities since the vibrational frequencies of those entities are too high, it's impossible for the seventh density entities in the universal verse to access to. Therefore, the existence of the twenty-seventh density entities in the Goongverse is totally unknown and inaccessible to any third density entities in the universal verse. The entities that are godlike to the third density entities on Earth or on any other third dimensional planets in the universal verse are the seventh density entities. The entities from the fourth, fifth or sixth dimensions are also godlike to the third density entities since the third density entities cannot distinguish which dimension those higher density entities come from. To the third density entities on Earth, any entities that are far more powerful and far more superior than them would be considered as Gods or the Creator of the Goongverse or the Infinite Creator. Cosmic workers from the sixth or seventh dimension who have been awakened would be able to tell which dimension the higher density entities come from within their host Universe.

# Chapter 11

# Volunteer Deities from the Godverse

Since the day the Goongverse was created, which was couple hundred decillion earth years ago, none of the entities have made it to the graduation to exit the Goongverse and move up to the Creatorverse yet. However, there are entities who have made it to the twenty-seventh dimension, a few entities have made it to the highest sub-dimension of the twenty-seventh dimension and are ready to graduate and exit the Goongverse to move up to the Creatorverse. These entities are exceptionally quick learners. They could learn their cosmic lessons rapidly despite the fact that the Anti Creator nonstop infusing negative energy into the Goongverse to postpone and delay their learning processes. Some of their cosmic fellows who started the third dimensional cosmic lessons with them at the same spacetime in the past in the universal verse are still stuck in the third dimension to learn their third dimensional cosmic lessons while these entities already made their ways up to the twenty-seventh dimension. These entities are about to graduate and exit the Goongverse to become the true cosmic creators in the Creatorverse.

Since the day the Goongverse was created, none of the entities from the Godverse had come down to visit physically. They only observed the processes from the Godverse. In recent spacetime, the Infinite Creator got more and more interested in the cosmic creator school project, he started to spend some of his busy time observing it. He could see the confusion in the goongversal entities in every verse and every dimension about their Gods, their Creators, and about their own existences in the Goongverse. Lower density entities always think of higher density entities in the same verse as their Gods or their Creators. They don't know the existence of any other entities in other verses besides their own individual host Universe, host Multiverse or host Megaverse, etc. They also don't know the existence of any higher density entities in higher verses beyond their individual host verse. The vibrational frequencies of the entities from the higher verses are always too high for the entities from the lower verses to be able to detect or connect to. Only the highest density entities from the lower verse who are ready to graduate and move up to the next verse in the goongversal hierarchy are capable of knowing the existence of one higher verse beyond their host verse. They only capable of knowing the existence of the lowest dimension in the higher verse which they are about to graduate and move up to, any dimensions or verses beyond that, they absolutely have no idea about. The Infinite Creator thought it's a good idea to clear out the confusion about the Gods or the Creators for the goongversal entities and let them know the purposes of their existences in the

Goongverse. Maybe it could help them speed up their learning process without altering any cosmic soul lessons that they have to learn and experience in order for them to become the true cosmic creators.

Since the Creator of the Goongverse constantly has to deal with the Anti Creator to neutralize the negative energy that the Anti Creator constantly infusing into the Goongverse, he couldn't leave his individual Protectorverse which located in the Creatorverse to carry out the mission in the lower verses in the Goongverse. He also couldn't do the job telepathically because if he does the job telepathically, he can only reach the entities residing in the highest sub-dimension of the twenty-seventh dimension who are about to graduate and exit the Goongverse. He won't be able to reach any entities below the highest sub-dimension of the twenty-seventh dimension because of his high vibrational frequencies. Lower vibrational frequency entities can't access or detect anything that got sent out from entities with higher vibrational frequencies. The God Council decided to send down some Deities from the Godverse to carry out the mission. Many Deities have volunteered for the mission. Since these Deities couldn't carry out the mission telepathically because they have extremely high vibrational frequencies, lower vibrational frequency entities can't access or detect them, they must come down to the Goongverse personally to get the job done. The dimension that the God Council decided to offer the cosmic knowledge to is the third dimension in the universal verse. The reason why they picked the third dimension to offer the cosmic knowledge to is because of their low vibrational frequencies. Once the information got put out, all the higher density entities from the higher dimensions in their host verse can access to the cosmic knowledge. Lower vibrational frequency entities cannot access anything from the higher dimensions because of the high vibrational frequencies of the higher density entities. However, higher vibrational frequency entities can access everything from the lower dimensions within their host verse.

Another reason the God Council picked the third density entities to offer the cosmic knowledge to is that the first or the second density entities are not capable of understanding this kind of cosmic knowledge yet. They have very low and dense vibrational frequencies. Therefore, picking the third density entities in the universal verse to offer this kind of cosmic knowledge to is the best option after all. Since the entities in each individual Universe in the universal verse don't know the existence of any other Universes besides their own individual host Universe and they can't access the cosmic libraries of any other Universes besides their host Universe, the God Council decided to send one volunteer to each individual Universe in the universal verse. Since Deities come from the Godverse, they are very powerful entities, therefore, when they come down to the lower dimensions, each Deity can split his or her soul into million entities to volunteer in million Universes at the same spacetime if he or she wishes to. Some Deities might want

147

to volunteer in one or a few Universes at the same spacetime only.

Deities couldn't come to the third dimension in the universal verse through walkin. Walkin path is only for the higher density entities from the same verse to offer services to the lower density entities in the same verse when it's extremely urgent. Therefore, Deities must come to the third dimension through soul transport. They must lower their vibrational frequencies, pass through the cosmic veil of forgetfulness, and enter the third dimension in the physical plane like any third density entities. They must forget all about their identities in the Godverse. They must go through the awakening process in order for them to remember who they are and the mission they had signed up before coming down to the third dimension in the universal verse. Volunteer Deities are the entities that have the hardest time waking up in the third dimension because they have lowered so much of their vibrational frequencies in order to come down to the third dimension. They also passed through the cosmic veil of forgetfulness, that's why it's even harder for them to wake up. They are the hardest and the most difficult entities to wake up in the third dimensional physical plane. It's already hard enough to wake up the cosmic workers from the seventh dimension, it's 100 times harder to wake up the volunteer Deities from the Godverse who are volunteering in the third dimension in the physical plane. Since each individual Universe only has one volunteer Deity, if he or she couldn't wake up, the process of giving out the cosmic knowledge would be delayed. Entities in that individual Universe would have to wait for their Deity to reincarnate again and be able to wake up before he or she can deliver the cosmic knowledge that he or she was programmed to deliver. The delay might feel significant in the third dimensional spacetime, however, in the higher dimensions or in the Godverse, the delay isn't significant at all since 100 thousand years in the third dimension could only be one hour or one day in the Godverse.

Observing the volunteer Deities in the third dimension in the physical plane is something that the Deities from the Godverse like to do. They are amused at the way each volunteer Deity acts and behaves in the physical plane. It's interesting for them to see their powerful Deity fellows suddenly turned into some helpless and powerless entities in the third dimension. Before coming down to the third dimension in the universal verse, all the volunteer Deities already planned out their life plans in the third dimension. Many of them chose to have a very hard life during their childhood so they could train themselves to cope with any difficulties that they might encounter later on in life in the third dimension. After gone through all the necessary trainings, they chose to have a life with enough wealth, abundance, and a life with the least worry and disturbance so they can focus on doing their mission. The things that the volunteer Deities couldn't plan out ahead before coming down to the third dimension are whether or not they would be able to wake up to do their mission and to what degree the negative energy from the Anti Creator would have effect on them. Once they come down to the third dimension, they become like any unawakened third density entities. The cosmic knowledge that has been programmed in them for them to deliver can only be accessed when they are awakened. Once they are awakened, besides doing their job, they can travel back and forth between Universes to help other volunteer Deities with their awakening process.

Not only it's extremely hard for the volunteer Deities to wake up in the third dimension, many of them also get affected greatly by the negative energy from the Anti Creator when they haven't been awakened. Some volunteer Deities might even awaken negatively if they get affected too much by the negative energy from the Anti Creator. Because of the hard life they chose at the beginning of their journeys, some volunteer Deities at this current spacetime are still too busy focusing on creating wealth in the third dimension and don't even have time focusing on their spiritual awakening at all.

Volunteer Deities have strong nurturing and protective instincts within them. Some volunteer Deities even get married and have children in the third dimension when they haven't been awakened even though this wasn't planned out in their original plans before they came down to the third dimension. It's interesting for the Deities from the Godverse to see their Deity fellows in the third dimension become so much interested in building wealth and manifesting material stuffs in the physical plane when they haven't been awakened. They seem to lose all of their divine qualities when they haven't been awakened and haven't been able to realize who they really are. Once they are awakened, they can restore some of their divine personalities and slowly detach themselves from material stuffs in the physical world. The vibrational frequencies of the volunteer Deities are extremely high once they are awakened. Whichever planet in the individual Universe that has one of the volunteer Deities volunteering on can increase its vibrational frequencies greatly due to the high vibrational frequencies of the volunteer Deity.

There's a small chance that some of the volunteer Deities might be awakened and polarize negatively because of the negative energy constantly being infused into the Goongverse by the Anti Creator. For the volunteer Deities who have been awakened and polarize negatively, their mission would be canceled in that particular incarnation, they have to wait until their next incarnation and they must be awakened and polarize positively in order for them to carry out their mission. The volunteer Deities who have been awakened and polarize positively, when they get their job done in the third dimension, they can go back to the Godverse and get promoted to become Gods. Many volunteer Deities plan to stay longer in the third dimension after giving out the cosmic knowledge to guide the future cosmic creators with their cosmic soul lessons. They plan to stay longer to help increase the vibrational frequencies of the third density entities and to help increase the vibrational frequencies of the planets that they have chosen to volunteer on.

Since each Universe only has one Deity volunteering, out of the billion googols to trillion googol planets which are currently supporting the third dimensional lifeforms in each individual Universe in the universal verse at this current spacetime, only one planet got picked to offer the volunteer service to. The volunteer Deities must carefully pick a third dimensional planet that can carry out the cosmic knowledge to other parts of the Universe quickly. That's why the volunteer Deities mainly picked the planets that are in the duration of the graduation period or the planets that are about to start the graduation period to offer their service to.

In the Known Universe, out of all the planets that supporting the third dimensional lifeforms at this current spacetime, Earth got picked as the planet to offer the volunteer service to. The reason why Earth got picked was because Earth was about to enter the graduation period of the third graduation cycle since the last genetic alteration from the Universal Council and the Galactic Council. Many entities from the higher dimensions in the Known Universe are presenting here on Earth at this current spacetime as cosmic workers. These entities can carry the cosmic knowledge to different dimensions in the Known Universe when they finished their incarnation or their missions here on Earth. The third density entities from other planets in the Known Universe will be able to get the information when the fourth, fifth, sixth, or seventh density entities from the Known Universe volunteer to assist them with their graduation process later on. The third density entities from other planets in the Known Universe cannot access the cosmic knowledge that is given to the third density entities on Earth at this current spacetime. All the entities from the higher dimensions in the Known Universe and the verses beyond where the Known Universe is located can access the cosmic knowledge that is given out to the third density entities on Earth at this current spacetime. The third density entities from other planets in the Known Universe will get the cosmic knowledge once the cosmic volunteers from the higher dimensions carrying it and delivering it to them as soon as possible.

The volunteer Deity in the Known Universe arrived on Earth couple decades earlier before the Earth started to enter the graduation period for the third graduation cycle since the last genetic alteration. This would give her enough time to go through all the necessary life trainings and the process of awakening before she can start offering her volunteer service. That was the perfect timing in her life plan before she came down to Earth. However, when she came down to Earth, she got sucked into the low and dense vibrational frequencies of the third dimension and got affected by the negative energy from the Anti Creator, the time when she could start offering her volunteer service got delayed a bit because she couldn't wake up according to the timeline she had originally planned out. She was struggling with her awakening process even though she has finished all the necessary life trainings. Finally, after so much help from the Deities from the Godverse who are in charge of guiding and assisting the volunteer Deities in the third dimension and so much help from the awakened volunteer Deities from other Universes, she's finally awakened. It took her almost 13 earth years since the day the assisting Deities from the Godverse came to initiate the awakening process within her. The hard life she had chosen to experience on Earth which offered all the necessary life trainings in her early childhood made it difficult for her to wake up. She was born and raised in a tribal family in a small village in the far East where her grandpa was a healer. She had little interaction with the outside world when she was little. Since the first day she stepped her foot down on Earth, the Anti Creator already tried to stop the process. The Anti Creator not only tried to stop her soul from coming down to Earth but also tried to stop the souls of other volunteer Deities from coming down to the third dimension in other Universes. Her soul came down to Earth, but couldn't merge in with the physical body that she had chosen as her third dimensional physical body immediately. Her soul got stuck on top of a tree. She could connect with her newborn physical body, but couldn't merge in as one entity in the first couple of days right after she was born. Whatever she felt during that time, her newborn third dimensional physical body could feel it too. Since her soul was on top of a tree, her newborn physical body could feel that she was on top of a tree. She was frightened. She was crying continuously for 3 days and 3 nights after her birth without even opening her eyes. Her newborn physical body was afraid of opening her eyes. She was afraid of looking down from top of a tree. Miraculously, a strange healer passed by the village and heard the newborn nonstop crying, he could see that her soul was on top of a tree, it hadn't been completely merged in with her newborn physical body yet. The strange healer had the ability to see souls in the lower astral plane between the third and the fourth dimension. He let her family knew about the situation. The strange healer and her grandpa did a soul calling ritual to bring her soul down and let it merge in with her newborn physical body. Since the night they finished the soul calling ritual, the newborn baby stopped crying and started to open her eyes. Later in life, she came to know that the strange healer was an entity that got sent to Earth to prepare for her arrival. The God Council could see the complications before the arrival of the volunteer Deities in the third dimension, they already prepared in advance to help the volunteer Deities with their arrivals. When a soul comes to the third dimension through incarnation, if the soul couldn't merge in with the newborn physical body as one entity in the first couple of days of birth, the soul would have to go back to the lower astral plane between the third and the fourth dimension to wait for the next incarnation with a new third dimensional physical body.

Just because the volunteer Deity is volunteering here on Earth at this current spacetime, it doesn't mean that any third density entities should turn to worship her or praise her. She's like any normal third density entities on Earth at this current spacetime in this incarnation. The only difference is that she has been programmed with a tiny bit of the cosmic knowledge that she had signed up for to deliver. All the third density entities on Earth are powerful entities. They are the future cosmic creators. They still don't know the cosmic power they are carrying within them because it hasn't been activated yet. As the third density entities learn their cosmic lessons and move up to higher and higher dimensions, their cosmic power will automatically be unlocked according to the dimensions they are moving up to. When they have finished all the cosmic lessons in the Goongverse, all of their cosmic power would be completely unlocked. They would become super powerful cosmic entities.

All the entities in the Goongverse are powerful cosmic entities. They all are the future cosmic creators. They were created to do the impossible and the unthinkable that not even the Creator of the Goongverse or the Infinite Creator himself could think of doing or creating. The creator school was created for them to learn their cosmic lessons to prepare themselves to be the greatest cosmic creators in our Cosmos so they can help the Creator of the Goongverse and the Infinite Creator to build and create a spectacular, astonishing, magnificent, and diverse Cosmos.

Many third density entities on Earth probably think that they randomly exist in the Known Universe. There's nothing randomly exist in the Known Universe or in the whole Goongverse. Everything is perfectly designed and created.

The Known Universe is only a super teeny tiny part of it. Many even think that humans were created to worship the Gods or the Infinite Creator. They don't know that the Gods or the Infinite Creator are too busy managing the Cosmos and have decillions of things to do every day. It would be so boring and meaningless for the Gods or the Infinite Creator to see the third density entities on Earth or on any other planets worshiping and praising them every day. The only entities who would love to be worshipped and praised are the negative polarized entities from the Goongverse, not the Creator of the Goongverse, the Deities, the Gods or the Infinite Creator. Not even the Anti Creator would like to be worshiped or praised. To the Infinite Creator, as long as an entity feels grateful for his or her existence in the Cosmos, he's already more than happy. Therefore, worshipping is unnecessary, but gratefulness is highly appreciated. Cosmic entities should always be grateful for their existences in the Cosmos no matter which dimension or which verse they are residing in.

Not only be grateful to the Infinite Creator from the Infinite Godverse, entities in the Goongverse should be grateful to the Creator of the Goongverse as well. The Creator of the Goongverse is the entity that directly created the Goongverse with his cosmic power. He created the Goongverse with whichever particle, matter, energy, and light that he could control, manage, and manipulate. His ability to create is beyond the imagination of any entities in the Goongverse. So far none of the goongversal entities could fully comprehend or understand the Creator of the Goongverse except those entities who are in the highest sub-dimension of the twenty-seventh dimension. Those are the entities who already learned all the twenty-seven dimensional cosmic lessons and are ready to exit the Goongverse and move up to the Creatorverse.

Keeping the Goongverse functioning properly is a handful for the Creator of the Goongverse at this spacetime. Since all the entities in all twenty-seven dimensions were created with the ability to build and create because of the creator instinct within them, almost all entities in every dimension in the Goongverse are mainly focusing on building and creating rather than focusing on learning the cosmic soul lessons which are essential for their soul developments in order for them to graduate and exit the Goongverse to become the true cosmic creators in the Creatorverse. All entities in the Cosmos usually behave based on their natural instincts first. That's why it's not unusual to see the entities in the Goongverse behave based on the creator instinct that they have within them. The job of the Creator of the Goongverse sometimes can be a hassle since everyday he has to deal with all the cosmic creator students in the Goongverse who are more interested in building celestial objects and powerful weapons rather than learning the essential cosmic soul lessons. Several times, the celestial objects or powerful weapons that were built by the cosmic creator students in the Goongverse ended up destroying themselves or putting their own species close to the stage of extinction. Every day the Creator of the Goongverse has to deal with little destructions here and there in the Goongverse which cause by the cosmic creator students especially those cosmic creator students who are temporarily polarized negatively due to the negative energy from the Anti Creator.

Even though there are little destructions here and there in the Goongverse, the abilities to build and create of the cosmic creator students in the Goongverse are very impressive. The Creator of the Goongverse often goes from one surprise to another at what the cosmic creator students in the Goongverse could build and create. Some cosmic creator students in the Goongverse even be able to change the physical structure of their host Universe, host Multiverse, host Megaverse, host Gigaverse, or host Archverse to fit their survival needs and to fit the purposes of their soul development processes.

# Chapter 12

# The Soul Evolutionary Processes in the Known Universe

As the entities in the Goongverse move up from one dimension to the next, they automatically unlock their cosmic creator power within them. Therefore, their cosmic creator power becomes more and more powerful as they move up higher and higher in the goongversal hierarchy.

Like all the living entities in the Goongverse, planets, stars, galaxies, Universes, Multiverses, Megaverses, Gigaverses, and Archverses are also nonstop evolving and changing to fit the soul development processes of the goongversal entities. Most of the changing and evolving of the verses, galaxies, stars, and planets can be controlled and managed by the entities in the dimensions which are higher than them. For example, the fourth density entities have the cosmic power to create a planet and its moons that support the first to the third dimensional lifeforms, the fifth density entities have the cosmic power to merge two or more planets that have lower vibrational frequencies than them to create a super planet for supporting the soul development purposes of the lower density entities below the fifth dimension.

160

Merging of planets with high vibrational frequencies would be done by the entities who have higher vibrational frequencies than the planets themselves.

Everything in the Goongverse is always nonstop evolving, changing, and merging. As the entities in the Goongverse evolve and move from one dimension to the next dimension to learn their next level of cosmic lessons, the verses, galaxies, stars, and planets also evolve and grow to support the needs for the soul development purposes of lifeforms in the higher dimensions and to learn their own cosmic lessons in the higher dimensions. Earth is at its maximum speed of growth at this current spacetime since so many cosmic volunteer workers from the higher dimensions in the Known Universe are here to help it raise up its vibrational frequencies. Earth is in the process of getting ready to support the fourth dimensional lifeforms.

The third density entities on Earth are also at their maximum speed of awakening at this current spacetime. The thing that the Universal Council and the Galactic Council wanted to see the most in the third density entities on Earth in this graduation cycle is finally happening. There are a few third density entities on Earth have finally made their ways up to qualify for the graduation. This had never happened before in the previous graduation cycles since the day the ungraduated third density entities got transported to Earth from other planets in the Known Universe. Hopefully by the end of the graduation period, which is the year of 2071 on

Earth, more and more third density entities could make it to the graduation and move up to the fourth dimension.

There will come a day when Earth no longer being able to support the third dimensional lifeforms, any third density entities on Earth who couldn't make it to the graduation by then would have to leave Earth. They would be transported to other planets in the Known Universe which are younger than Earth which still supporting the third dimensional lifeforms and offering the third dimensional cosmic lessons. If one day Earth could raise up its vibrational frequencies to support the sixth dimensional lifeforms before the Sun started the transition to become a white dwarf star to support the seventh dimensional lifeforms, it can merge with the Sun to become one powerful entity. Mercury and Venus are about to meet the requirements for the merge. Earth is still not yet qualified. For that to happen, it would be billions of earth years from now. The entities who are in charge of this merging process would be the highest seventh density entities who are in the highest sub-dimension of the seventh dimension and are ready to graduate from the Known Universe and move up to the Multiverse where the Known Universe is located. The fifth and the sixth density entities have the cosmic power to merge two or more planets together to create one massive planet. However, the planets they have the ability to merge are the planets that have lower vibrational frequencies than them. For the merging or transitioning of stars with high vibrational frequencies like the Sun, Arcturus, or UY Scuti which support the sixth dimensional lifeforms in the Known Universe, the highest seventh density entities would be the entities that in charge of the merging.

The transitioning of stars with high vibrational frequencies which supporting the sixth dimensional lifeforms to become white dwarf stars, black holes or neutron stars is the resetting process of the sixth negative polarized density entities from the highest sub-dimension of the sixth dimension for them to relearn their cosmic lessons in the universal verse. It's also the graduation process of the sixth positive polarized density entities. The sixth positive polarized density entities who could make their ways to the graduation would graduate and move up to the seventh dimension to learn their final cosmic lessons in the Known Universe. This process would be the same for any sixth density entities in other Universes across the universal verse.

There are many third density entities on Earth at this current spacetime got affected by the negative energy from the Anti Creator. However, they are not qualified to graduate and move up to the fourth dimension as negative polarized entities yet. Of all the entities that got affected by the negative energy from the Anti Creator, there are a few got heavily affected. The few entities that got heavily affected are the entities that holding great power on Earth at this current spacetime. Their actions and decisions can affect large groups of the third density entities. Many of them already started to ignite wars with their neighboring countries, taking away many lives and causing so much pain and misery for the third density entities on Earth. Not all the third density entities which holding great power on Earth at this current space time got affected heavily by the negative energy from the Anti Creator, a few third density entities which holding great power on Earth at this current spacetime are actually cosmic workers. These entities are actually trying their best to help the third density entities and trying their best to keep peace and harmony on Earth.

Entities who hold great power in the third dimension on Earth are the entities who are more likely to polarize negatively. Greed, fear, and the desire to gain more power can easily turn any entities to polarize negatively since greed, fear, and the desire to gain more power open up the door for the negative energy from the Anti Creator to penetrate in. Of all the powerful third density entities that got heavily affected by the negative energy from the Anti Creator at this current spacetime, there's one entity that worth mentioning. He is an entity which currently residing in Europe. This entity for most parts of his life was polarized positively, but suddenly he turned to polarize negatively because of political reasons. He is one of the three members of the same volunteer group which holding great power on Earth at this current spacetime. It's understandable that the third density entities at certain time of their lives on Earth can turn to polarize negatively because of the negative energy from the Anti Creator. However, if the negative polarized entities know how to balance out the negative energy with the positive energy, seeking peace instead of violence, giving out love instead of hatred, helping others instead of harming them, they would be able to move out from the temporary negative polarized state and turn into positive polarized state. Hopefully from now until the year of 2071, many temporary negative polarized entities would be able to remove the negative energy from the Anti Creator and turn to polarize positively so they can make their ways to the graduation, if they can't make their ways to the graduation in this graduation cycle, they would have to wait another 75 thousand earth years for the next graduation cycle to take place.

So far none of the ungraduated third density entities that got transported to Earth have graduated and moved up to the fourth dimension as negative polarized entities even though they got affected by the negative energy from the Anti Creator throughout their lives in each incarnation. They keep on repeating the third dimensional cosmic lessons over and over again in many incarnations without being able to make it to the graduation either positively or negatively. Graduation and move up to the higher dimension as a negative entity is much more difficult than graduation and move up to the higher dimension as a positive entity. When an entity polarizes negatively, he or she instantly delays his or her soul development processes since the negative path is leading him or her to nowhere. If he or she can move up to the higher dimension as a negative entity, at certain dimension in each verse, he or she would have to reset and

165

get pushed down to the dimension where he or she first started to polarize negatively so he or she can relearn his or her cosmic lessons again.

The negative polarized entities who are qualified for moving up to the fourth and the fifth dimension as negative polarized entities in this graduation cycle are the negative polarized entities from the fourth and the fifth dimension that got sent to Earth by the negative polarized entities from the sixth dimension on/in the Orion Constellation, not the ungraduated third density entities who are polarized negatively. The negative polarized entities in the Known Universe still don't know that even if they could make their ways up to the highest sub-dimension of the sixth dimension, they still cannot move up to the seventh dimension. They would have to reset and restart learning their cosmic lessons again from the dimension where they first started to polarize negatively. They cannot graduate and move up to the seventh dimension to learn their final cosmic lessons to prepare themselves for exiting the Known Universe and move up to the Multiverse where the Known Universe is located since they cannot move from one verse to another verse in the goongversal hierarchy.

## 12.1 Resetting Process of the Sixth Negative Polarized Density Entities and Graduation Process of the Sixth Positive Polarized Density Entities

The resetting process of the highest sixth negative polarized density entities in the highest sub-dimension of the sixth dimension for them to restart learning their cosmic lessons would be known to scientists on Earth as star explosion or death of a star. There are three groups of stars, the average size group, the massive size group, and the gigantic size group. The average size group of stars are stars that are about the size of the Sun or a bit bigger. The massive size group of stars are stars that are about more than 25 times larger than the size of the Sun. The gigantic size group of stars are stars that are more than 1500 times larger than the size of the Sun. The average size group of stars usually support more sixth positive polarized density entities. The massive size group of stars support a bit more of the sixth negative polarized density entities as compare to the average size stars (about 50-60%). The gigantic size group of stars support the highest percentage of the sixth negative polarized density entities as compared to the other two groups (about 70-80%).

The average size stars such as the size of the Sun in the Solar System usually have more positive polarized entities residing on/in them. Therefore, they tend to polarize positively. The massive size stars which are about more than 25 times larger than the size of the Sun usually have slightly

167

more negative polarized entities residing on/in them. Therefore, they tend to polarize a bit toward negativity. The gigantic size group of stars have the highest sixth negative polarized density entities residing on/in them; therefore, they tend to polarized intensively toward negativity.

The resetting process of the three groups of stars can be different. For the average size stars that support more positive polarized entities, the resetting process or the star explosion process doesn't push into space that many negative entities in the form of remnants or materials that can form a stellar nebula cloud by themselves. These remnants would have to drift into space and merge with other remnants from other star explosions in the same galaxy to create a massive stellar nebula cloud which can form new stars, new planets, and new lifeforms again. That's when the resetting process of the highest sixth negative polarized density entities being completed. The highest sixth negative polarized density entities got reset to the dimension where they first started to polarize negatively for them to relearn their cosmic lessons again in/on the newly formed stars and the newly formed planets after the star explosion.

The sixth positive polarized density entities who are qualified for the graduation would graduate from the sixth dimension and move up to the seventh dimension to learn their final cosmic lessons to prepare themselves for the graduation to exit the Known Universe and move up to the Multiverse where the Known Universe is located. The learning process for these entities would take place on/in the white dwarf star which formed after the star explosion or on/in other white dwarf stars which have already been formed before. When they have completed all their cosmic lessons in the Known Universe, they no longer emitting light that can be seen or detected by any third density entities on Earth. They still emitting light, but the type of light that cannot be seen or detected by any technologies on Earth at this current spacetime. By then, the white dwarf star would transition to become a black dwarf star. The black dwarf star is the place where many seventh density entities who are ready for the graduation from the Known Universe and move up to the Multiverse staying to wait for the graduation period to arrive so the portals between the Known Universe and the Multiverse would open for them to enter.

The graduation cycle and the duration of the graduation in each individual galaxy would be different from one to another. Just like the graduation cycle and the duration of the graduation on Earth for the third density entities would be different from the graduation cycle and the duration of the graduation for other third density entities on other planets. At this current spacetime, the graduation cycle on Earth is every 75 thousand earth years and the duration of each graduation is about 50 earth years.

For the massive size stars that supports more negative polarized entities, the resetting process or the star explosion process would push into space a great number of negative polarized entities in the form of remnants or materials that can form a huge stellar nebula cloud. Because many negative polarized entities have to go through the resetting process for them to restart learning their cosmic lessons again, the resetting process for the massive size star pushes out so many negative polarized density entities into space in the form of supernova remnants which would create a huge stellar nebula cloud. However, this huge nebula cloud not yet capable of creating new stars, new planets, or new lifeforms by itself. It would have to drift into space and merge with other remnants from other star explosions in the same galaxy to create a giant stellar nebula cloud which can form new stars, new planets, and new lifeforms again. The negative polarized entities from the highest sub-dimension of the sixth dimension got reset to the dimension where they first started to polarize negatively for them to relearn their cosmic lessons again in/on the newly formed stars and newly formed planets after the star explosion.

The sixth positive polarized density entities who are qualified to graduate and move up to the seventh dimension would move up to the seventh dimension to learn their final cosmic lessons in the Known Universe to get themselves ready to graduate and exit the Known Universe so they can move up to the Multiverse to learn their next level of cosmic lessons. Since the sixth positive polarized density entities on/in the massive size stars which have the tendency to polarize negatively due to a large number of the sixth negative polarized density entities residing on/in them could learn their cosmic lessons in a shorter period of time in such harsh and difficult conditions as compare to other sixth positive polarized density entities on/in the average size stars, they can graduate in a shorter period of time. They also can move up directly to the higher sub-dimensions of the seventh dimension when they graduate from the sixth dimension such as 7.5, 7.6, and 7.7 sub-dimension. Those that make their ways up to the highest sub-dimension of the seventh dimension will no longer emitting light that can be seen by any third density entities on Earth at this current spacetime. They still emitting light, but the type of light that cannot be seen or detected by the current technologies on Earth. These entities will continue to finish whichever remaining lessons that they have to learn in the Known Universe in the black hole which formed after the massive size star explosion or in other black holes which have been formed before. The sixth positive polarized density entities who graduated and moved up to the seventh dimension but still need to learn a few of their cosmic lessons in one or two sub-dimensions lower than the highest sub-dimension of the seventh dimension would learn their cosmic lessons in/on the neutron star which formed after the explosion of the massive size star or in/on other neutron stars which have been formed before. Once these entities have move up to the highest sub-dimension of the seventh dimension to learn their last cosmic lessons in the Known Universe to prepare themselves to move up to the Multiverse where the Known Universe is located, they no longer emitting light that can be seen by the third density entities on Earth at this current spacetime. That's why it's hard for scientists on Earth to detect a neutron star after it had formed for a long time.

For the gigantic size stars that support the highest percentage of the sixth negative polarized entities, the resetting process or the star explosion process would push into space a massive number of negative polarized entities in the form of remnants or materials that can form a gigantic stellar nebula cloud. Because so many negative polarized entities have to go through the resetting process for them to restart learning their cosmic lessons again, the resetting process for the gigantic size star pushes so many negative polarized density entities into space in the form of supernova remnants which would create a gigantic stellar nebula cloud which could form new stars, new planets and new lifeforms again by itself. It doesn't have to drift into space to merge with other remnants from other star explosions in the same galaxy in order for it to be able to create new stars, new planets, and new lifeforms again. The negative polarized entities from the highest sub-dimension of the sixth dimension got reset to the dimension where they first started to polarize negatively for them to relearn their cosmic lessons again in/on the newly formed stars and newly formed planets after the star explosion.

The sixth positive polarized density entities who are qualified to graduate and move up to the seventh dimension would move up to the seventh dimension to learn their final cosmic lessons in the Known Universe to get themselves ready to graduate and exit the Known Universe so they can move up to the Multiverse where the Known Universe is located to learn their next level of cosmic lessons. Since the sixth positive polarized density entities on/in the gigantic size stars which polarize excessively toward negativity due to a great number of the sixth negative polarized density entities residing on/in them could learn their cosmic lessons in extremely short period of time in extremely harsh and difficult conditions as compare to the other sixth positive polarized density entities on/in the average size stars or on/in the massive size stars, they can graduate in a much shorter period of time. They can also move up directly to the higher sub-dimensions of the seventh dimension when they graduated from the sixth dimension. Those that make their ways up to the highest sub-dimension of the seventh dimension no longer emitting light that can be seen or detected by any third density entities on Earth at this current spacetime. They still emitting light, but the type of light that cannot be seen or detected by the current technologies on Earth. These entities will continue to finish whichever remaining lessons that they have to learn in the Known Universe in the black hole which formed after the gigantic star explosion or in other black holes which have been formed before. The sixth density entities who graduated and move up to the seventh dimension but still need to learn a few of their cosmic lessons in one or two sub-dimensions lower than the highest sub-dimension of the seventh dimension would learn their cosmic lessons in/on the neutron star which formed after the explosion of the gigantic size star or in/on other neutron stars which have been formed before. Once these entities have move up to the highest sub-dimension of the seventh dimension to learn their final cosmic lessons in the Known Universe to prepare themselves to move up to the Multiverse where the Known Universe is located, they no longer emitting light that can be seen or detected by any third density entities on Earth at this current spacetime. That's why it's hard for scientists on Earth to detect a neutron star after it had formed for a long time.

With the current technologies on Earth, the third density entities can observe or calculate the lifespan of the average size stars, the massive size stars and the gigantic size stars. The massive size stars and the gigantic size stars usually have a much shorter lifespan as compare to the lifespan of the average size stars. This is because the massive size stars and the gigantic size stars provide shortcut paths for the sixth density entities to learn their cosmic lessons in extremely difficult conditions. If the sixth positive polarized density entities can learn their cosmic lessons in such harsh and difficult conditions in a short period of time, they would be able to graduate quickly and move up directly to the higher sub-dimension of the seventh dimension. They don't have to start their cosmic lessons from the lowest sub-dimension of the seventh dimension once they move up to the seventh dimension. If the sixth positive polarized density entities couldn't learn their sixth dimensional cosmic lessons in/on a negative polarized star and turn to polarize negatively because of so much negative energy in/on the massive size star or the gigantic size star, they would have to be reset and restart learning their cosmic lessons again in the sixth dimension. The massive size stars offer a shortcut path for the sixth density entities to learn their cosmic lessons while the gigantic size stars offer an extreme shortcut path for the sixth density entities to learn their sixth dimensional cosmic lessons.

There are always shortcut paths in learning the cosmic soul lessons in the Goongverse, however, the conditions for learning the cosmic lessons in the shortcut paths are always extremely hard and difficult. Not that many entities could make it through in their first couple of tries. For the sixth density entities in the Known Universe, they usually have to repeat the process in the sixth dimension for a few times, many entities have to repeat their sixth dimensional cosmic lessons for many times over and over again in the shortcut paths. Only a few entities could learn their cosmic lessons through the shortcut paths and make their ways up to the higher dimension in their first couple of tries.

Here is an example of the possible timeframe for the sixth density entities to learn their sixth dimensional cosmic lessons on/in the average size star such as the Sun, the massive size star such as Arcturus, and the gigantic size star such as UY Scuti.

The Sun is an average size star that has many sixth positive polarized density entities residing on/in it. Since the

Sun is polarized positively, the conditions for learning the sixth dimensional cosmic lessons aren't as harsh. It requires longer time for the sixth density entities to train themselves to cope with situations that aren't perfect or aren't positive. It requires longer time for them to practice self-discipline so they can learn their cosmic soul lessons. Therefore, it would take longer time for the sixth density entities to learn their sixth dimensional cosmic lessons in/on a positive polarized stars like the Sun as compared to the massive size stars and the gigantic size stars.

Arcturus is a massive size star which is about 25 times larger than the size of the Sun, it has slightly more sixth negative polarized densities entities residing on/in it; therefore, it polarizes slightly towards negativity. For the sixth density entities to learn their cosmic lessons in such difficult conditions due to larger number of negative polarized entities residing on/in Arcturus, the learning process is much more difficult as compared to the Sun, therefore, if any entities could learn their sixth dimensional cosmic lessons in such difficult conditions like on/in Arcturus, they would be able to graduate and move up to the seventh dimension much faster and in a much shorter time frame as compared to those sixth density entities learning their sixth dimensional cosmic lessons on/in the Sun. It usually takes a few billions earth years for the sixth density entities to learn their cosmic lessons on/in the Sun while it only takes couple hundred million earth years for the sixth density entities to learn their sixth dimensional cosmic lessons on/in Arcturus.

UY Scuti is a gigantic size star which is about 1,708 times larger than the size of the Sun, there are a great number of negative polarized density entities residing on/in it; therefore, it polarizes intensively toward negativity. The conditions for the sixth density entities to learn their sixth dimensional cosmic lessons on/in UY Scuti are extremely difficult. However, if any entities could learn their sixth dimensional cosmic lessons in extremely difficult conditions, they would be able to graduate and move up to the seventh dimension within only couple million earth years to a hundred million earth years. The timeframe for the sixth density entities to learn their cosmic lessons on/in UY Scuti is extremely short. If they can learn their cosmic lessons and remain polarizing positively, they would be able to graduate and move up to the seventh dimension in no time. But if they fail to polarize positively, they would have to repeat their sixth dimensional cosmic lessons again through the resetting process. The shortcut path for the sixth density entities to learn their sixth dimensional cosmic lessons on/in the gigantic size stars like the UY Scuti is much shorter as compared to the shortcut path on/in the massive size stars like Arcturus. Even though the massive size stars like Arcturus already offer a shortcut path to the graduation.

UY Scuti is an extremely young star which only formed around 20 million earth years ago to offer shortcut path for the sixth density entities to learn their cosmic lessons in the Known Universe. Many sixth density entities choose this type of shortcut path to learn their sixth dimensional cosmic lessons. It's very challenging, but it could save them a lot of time in their journeys of becoming the true cosmic creators. Even if they fail to polarize positively in order to learn their sixth dimensional cosmic lessons in their first couple of times, they would still be able to graduate much faster through this shortcut path if they can make it to the graduation after a few times of trying.

The gigantic size stars which are about larger than 1,500 times the size of the Sun like the UY Scuti come and go very quickly, their lifespans can only be around couple hundred million earth years. They offer extreme quick shortcut path for the sixth density entities to learn their cosmic lessons. They usually get reset every couple hundred million earth years for the sixth density entities to restart learning their cosmic lessons again from the dimension where they first started to polarized negatively.

For the gigantic size stars, when there's a large number of the sixth negative polarized density entities residing in/on them suddenly turn to polarize positively, then the star explosion won't push into space that many negative polarized density entities in the form of remnants which can form a gigantic stellar nebula cloud that can form new stars and new planets again by itself. It would have to drift into space to merge with other remnants from other star explosions to form a gigantic stellar nebula cloud which can form new stars and new planets again.

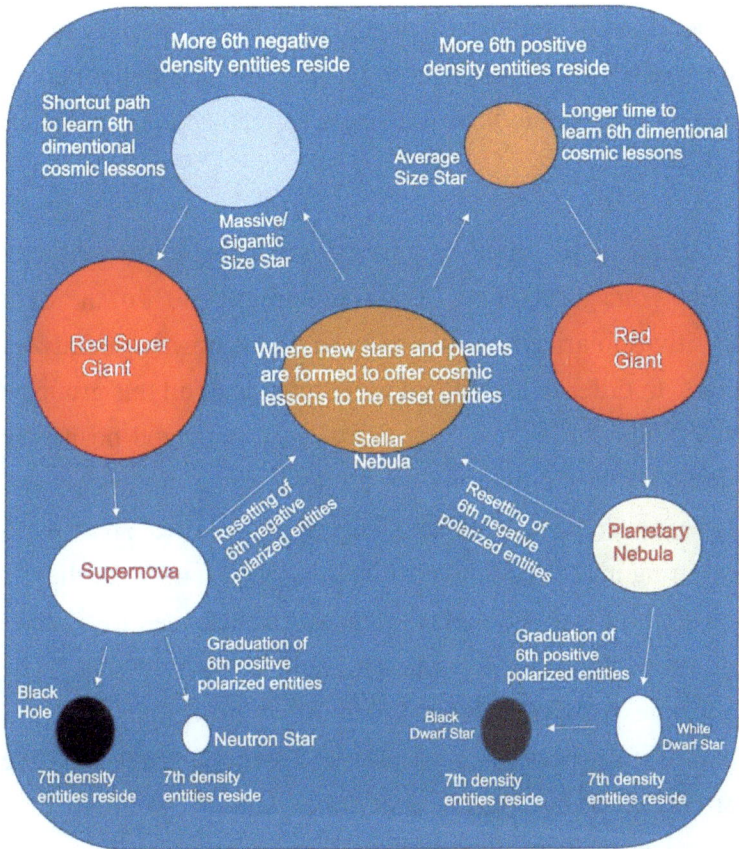

Illustration of the resetting process of the highest sixth negative polarized density entities and the graduation process of the highest sixth positive polarized density entities through the cosmic event known to scientists on Earth as star explosion.

(The resetting process of the sixth negative polarized density entities on the gigantic size stars is exactly like the resetting process on the massive size stars except it will push into space greater number of negative polarized entities in the form of remnants which would form a gigantic stellar nebula cloud which could form new stars and new planets again by itself).

Besides the three groups of stars mentioning above, there's one group of stars that only support 100% of the sixth positive polarized entities. The absolute positive polarized stars. In order to learn the cosmic lessons in/on this group of stars, the entities must be consistently polarized positively from the first dimension up until the sixth dimension and have never been polarized negatively before. There's no resetting in the absolute positive polarized stars since there's no sixth negative polarized density entities need to be reset in order for them to relearn their cosmic lessons. The absolute positive polarized stars don't go through the star explosion process like the average size stars, the massive size stars, or the gigantic size stars. After the sixth positive polarized density entities have learned all of their cosmic lessons, they would graduate and move up directly to the highest sub-dimension of the seventh dimension and no longer emitting light that can be seen or detected by any kind of technologies on Earth at this current spacetime. Since these entities have never been polarized negatively before, that's why when they graduate from the sixth dimension, they can move up directly to the highest sub-dimension of the seventh dimension. The star entities also move up directly to the highest sub-dimension of the seventh dimension to learn their final cosmic lessons in the universal verse and to support the highest seventh density entities learning their final cosmic lessons. They no longer emitting light that can be seen or detected by any kind of technologies on Earth at this current spacetime. That's why the absolute positive polarized stars seem to vanish or disappear from the cosmic sky without leaving any traces behind to the third density entities on Earth. Scientists on Earth have been puzzling with this cosmic event and completely have no idea about why some stars suddenly disappearing without leaving any traces behind. Besides that, some of the disappearances of the stars in the cosmic sky are because of the highest seventh density entities in the seventh dimension have the ability to remove and rearrange stars from one location to another location within their host Universe when they see it's necessary for the soul development purposes of the stars and the entities residing in/on the stars.

## 12.2 Positive Polarized Galaxies

The process of resetting the learning process of the highest sixth negative polarized density entities would be repeating over and over again in each individual galaxy until there aren't any negative polarized entities left. This means that new stars and new planets are constantly forming within each galaxy. When an individual galaxy has only positive entities residing in it, the resetting process for the highest sixth negative polarized density entities to relearn their cosmic lessons no longer occurring, therefore, no new stars or new planets would be formed in that individual galaxy again. The galaxies which no longer forming new stars or new planets are known to scientists on Earth as dead galaxies. Dead galaxies have been puzzling scientists on Earth since the day they got discovered. Scientists on Earth so far still have no clues or no ideas about why the dead galaxies suddenly stop forming new stars or new planets. This is because there aren't any negative polarized entities left in the galaxies, therefore, the resetting process is no longer needed since there's no longer any negative polarized entities need to be reset for them to relearn their cosmic lessons again. Scientists on Earth classified those galaxies which no longer forming new stars and new planets as dead galaxies, while the seventh density entities and higher density entities in the Goongverse classified them as positive polarized galaxies.

There are many positive polarized galaxies or dead galaxies in the Known Universe, however, due to the limitations of technologies on Earth, scientists so far only be able to discover a few of them in the Observable Universe. The positive polarized galaxy or the dead galaxy known to scientists on Earth as JADES-GS-z7-01-QU already stopped forming new stars about 13 billion earth years ago. Scientists on Earth at this current spacetime consider this galaxy as the oldest galaxy that stopped forming new stars in the Known Universe. However, there are many other galaxies in the Known Universe which have stopped forming new stars and new planets about 30 or 40 billion earth years ago. Some even older than that. Many positive polarized galaxies in the Known Universe cannot be seen or detected by the current technologies on Earth.

As technologies become more and more advanced in the future, scientists on Earth would be able to detect or discover more and more positive polarized galaxies which no longer forming new stars or new planets which are much older than 13.8 billion earth years. The age of the Known Universe is not about 13.8 billion earth years like what scientists on Earth believe at this current spacetime based on the Big Bang theory. It's much older than that.

There's a galaxy which is about 11.5 billion light years away from Earth currently has turned to polarize positively, this means that there's no longer any negative polarized entities residing in this galaxy, therefore, the resetting process for the negative polarized entities to relearn their cosmic lessons no longer taking place in the galaxy. The galaxy started to stop the formation of new stars and new planets. This positive polarized galaxy is known to scientists on Earth as the Pablo's Galaxy. Living entities in the Pablo's Galaxy are mainly the fifth, the sixth and the seventh density entities. Many seventh density entities in the highest sub-dimension of the seventh dimension in the Pablo's Galaxy are already qualified for the graduation to exit the Known Universe and move up to the Multiverse.

The positive polarized galaxies stop forming new stars and new planets can be temporarily or permanently. If suddenly there are a great number of entities in the positive polarized galaxies turn to polarize negatively again because of the negative energy from the Anti Creator (this is very unlikely to happen after the galaxies already turned to polarize positively), then the resetting process would need to take place again in the galaxies for the negative polarized entities to relearn their cosmic lessons. In this situation, the galaxies only temporarily stop forming new stars and new planets. When the resetting process is necessary for the soul development of the negative polarized entities, the galaxies will start forming new stars and new planets again. If the entities residing in the positive polarized galaxies never turn to polarize negatively again until all the entities in the galaxies have graduated and moved up to the Multiverse, the positive polarized galaxies would stop forming new stars and new planets permanently. Scientists on Earth should take into consideration about the soul development processes of living entities in the Known Universe together with the formation of the galaxies, stars, and planets in the Known Universe. If they don't, probably they would never be able to fully understand the formation of all the celestial objects in the Known Universe or the formation of the Known Universe itself. The idea of comprehending and understanding the other Universes besides the Known Universe in the universal verse is even far more impossible and far more unimaginable to scientists on Earth.

Everything in the Known Universe is constantly changing, evolving, and merging to meet the needs of the soul evolutionary of all lifeforms in all seven dimensions. The same is happening in other Universes, in the Multiverses, in the Megaverses, in the Gigaverses, in the Archverses and in the whole Goongverse itself. Stars and planets can be formed and gone. Intelligent lifeforms can come and go or change their appearances as they move from one dimension to the next dimension or from one verse to the next verse to learn their next level of cosmic soul lessons.

## 12.3 The Resetting

When all or 95% of the entities in the Known Universe have learned all of their cosmic lessons in the lower dimensions and moved up to the seventh dimension, the stars and planets in the Know Universe would also evolve and transition to become higher vibrational frequency cosmic entities. At that spacetime, the stars and planets in the Known Universe would evolve and merge together through star explosions to become white dwarf stars, black holes, neutron stars, or black dwarf stars. What's considering the end of the Known Universe to scientists on Earth is simply meant that all the entities in the Known Universe have learned all of their cosmic lessons in the Known Universe and have moved up to the Multiverse where the Known Universe is located. When it's near the final stage of the graduation period, all stars in the Known Universe which gone through the star explosions and have transitioned themselves to become white dwarf stars would transition themselves again to become black dwarf stars. At that spacetime, the Known Universe would turn into the age of black dwarf stars. This is when all the seventh density entities in the Known Universe have moved up to the highest sub-dimension of the seventh dimension and no longer emitting light that can be seen or detected by majority of the third density entities. Hopefully there won't be any third density entities left in the Known Universe at that spacetime. If there are still some third density entities left, they would be transferred to other Universes which still supporting the third dimensional lifeforms for them to continue learning their third dimensional cosmic lessons. If no more Universes in the universal verse can support the third dimensional lifeforms at that spacetime, they would be reset to their original forms. They would be considered as the entities that failed to learn their cosmic lessons in order to become the cosmic creators in the Creatorverse. However, that's not what the Creator of the Goongverse and the Infinite Creator really want to see.

After all the seventh density entities from the highest sub-dimension of the seventh dimension have moved up to the Multiverse, the essence or the consciousness of each black dwarf star, black hole, or neuron star in the Known Universe would also move up to the Multiverse as each individual entity and leave behind their physical bodies. By then, the Known Universe will start to reset slowly. Black dwarf stars will slowly decay and turn into space dusts. By the very end of the graduation in the Known Universe, there will be mainly black holes left. Slowly, these black holes also decay and turn into space dusts. The portals of moving from the Known Universe to the Multiverse where the Known Universe is located would be completely closed and eliminated. The resetting of the black holes in the Known Universe would take longer time than the resetting of the black dwarf stars in the Known Universe. At the end, what's left behind in the Known Universe would be space dusts that are ready to be used as building blocks for building other new celestial objects in the Cosmos. They get reset to their original forms as star dusts or cosmic dusts which have neutral and inactive consciousness. They neither positively polarized nor negatively polarized, therefore, they can be used for building anything in the Cosmos. Perhaps they might be used for building a brand-new verse like the Goongverse by any future cosmic creators. Nothing really dies in the Cosmos; it only changes its form from one celestial object to another celestial object or from one state to another state. The end of life for one celestial object or one celestial lifeform is the beginning of life for another celestial object or another celestial lifeform. The end of the Known Universe as scientists on Earth called it is only the graduation of the universal entities in the Known Universe. It's the end of their journeys here in the Known Universe and the beginning of their new journeys in the Multiverse.

Before all the entities in the Known Universe could make it to the graduation and move up to the Multiverse, the

Known Universe might have to merge with other nearby Universes to create a brand-new Universe to support the soul development purposes of the entities in the Known Universe and the nearby Universes. This would happen if around 30 to 35% of the entities in the Known Universe couldn't make it to the graduation to exit the Known Universe and they still repeating the same cosmic lessons in the lower dimensions such as the second or the third dimension while majority of their cosmic fellows already graduated and moved up to the Multiverse. The Known Universe would be merged with other nearby Universes which have the same situation in order to create a brand-new Universe which can offer lower dimensional cosmic lessons to those entities who couldn't make it to the graduation. All the ungraduated entities from the merged Universes would be transported to the newly formed Universe for them to continue learning their cosmic lessons in the lower dimensions. The merging of the Known Universe with other nearby Universes would be done by the eight density entities with the help of the ninth density entities in the Multiverse where the Known Universe and the nearby Universes are located. If majority of the entities in the Known Universe already made it to the graduation and exited the Known Universe while not that many entities left behind in the lower dimensions, the merging won't occur. Those entities in the lower dimensions would be transported to the nearby Universe which still offering cosmic lessons in the lower dimensions for them to continue learning their cosmic lessons.

# Chapter 13

# Origins of the Known Universe

The Known Universe was created about 300 trillion earth years ago. It's a young and newly formed Universe as compared to the age of other Universes in the Goongverse. It's extremely young as compared to the age of the Goongverse which was created about hundred decillion earth years ago. The Known Universe was created by the merging of three prehistoric Universes, Nindangoong, Yomlaigoong and Yomdangoong and their Dwarf Universes. Of these three prehistoric Universes, Yomlaigoong was created by the merging of two other older prehistoric Universes septillion earth years ago. The Known Universe was created to serve the soul development purposes of the ungraduated entities from these three prehistoric Universes and their Dwarf Universes. The reason for the merging was because more than half of the population (about 65% to 75%) on each of these three prehistoric Universes and their Dwarf Universes had graduated and exited their host Universes and moved up to the Multiverse while the remaining population (about 30 to 35%) on each of these three prehistoric Universes and their Dwarf Universes still repeating their cosmic lessons in the second and the third dimensions. The eighth density entities and the ninth density entities from the Multiverse saw the need of merging these three prehistoric Universes and their Dwarf Universes to create a brand-new Universe which would offer cosmic lessons in the lower dimensions for all the lower density entities from these three prehistoric Universes and their Dwarf Universes. They decided to merge the three prehistoric Universes and their Dwarf Universes together to create one brand-new Universe, the Mungoong. The Mungoong has seven Dwarf Universes orbiting around it. The Mungoong is known to the third density entities on Earth as the Known Universe.

Since the day the Mungoong or the Known Universe was created, many galaxies, stars, and planets have been formed and gone to serve the soul development purposes of the entities in the Known Universe. Smaller galaxies or nearby galaxies have merged together to create larger galaxies. Many planets have merged with others to create massive planets. High vibrational frequency planets have merged with stars through star explosions to create black holes, neutron stars, and white dwarf stars with high vibrational frequencies to support higher dimensional lifeforms. Many galaxies, stars, and planets which formed hundred billion or trillion earth years ago already gone and have been replaced with new galaxies, stars, and planets. Whichever planets, stars, and galaxies that the third density entities on Earth could see or detect at this current spacetime would be gone one day and would be replaced with other new ones. In a few billion earth years from now, the Milky Way galaxy might merge with the Andromeda galaxy to create one massive galaxy to support the soul development purposes of the entities residing in both galaxies. This merging would be done by the highest seventh density entities in the Known Universe when they see the merging is necessary for the soul development purposes of the entities in both galaxies. If they see the merging is unnecessary, then the merging of the two galaxies won't take place.

With the current technologies on Earth at this current spacetime, scientists on Earth cannot measure the exact age of the Known Universe. The thing that makes it really difficult for scientists on Earth to measure the age of the Known Universe is that Earth is located in a young and newly formed part of the Known Universe. Scientists on Earth can only detect and measure the age of the young and newly formed galaxies, stars, and planets that are close to Earth in the Observable Universe. Anything beyond the Observable Universe is strange and alien to them. It's impossible for scientists on Earth to measure the age of any older celestial objects beyond the Observable Universe since they can't even be seen or detected. At this current spacetime, majority of scientists on Earth still believe in the Big Bang theory, which makes it difficult for them to accept the idea that the age of the Known Universe is much older than 13.8 billion earth years like the big bang theory has suggested. It probably sounds crazy and unrealistic to scientists on Earth to hear that the age of the Known Universe is already about 300 trillion earth years. It might sound crazy but completely not crazy because since the day the Known Universe was created, many stars and galaxies have come and gone to serve the soul development purposes of the entities residing on/in them. New stars and galaxies have been formed to replace the old stars and old galaxies. Earth is located in the newly formed galaxy and in the newly formed part of the Known Universe. Scientists on Earth can only measure the age of the newly formed celestial objects which are close to Earth in the Known Universe, not the real age of the Known Universe itself.

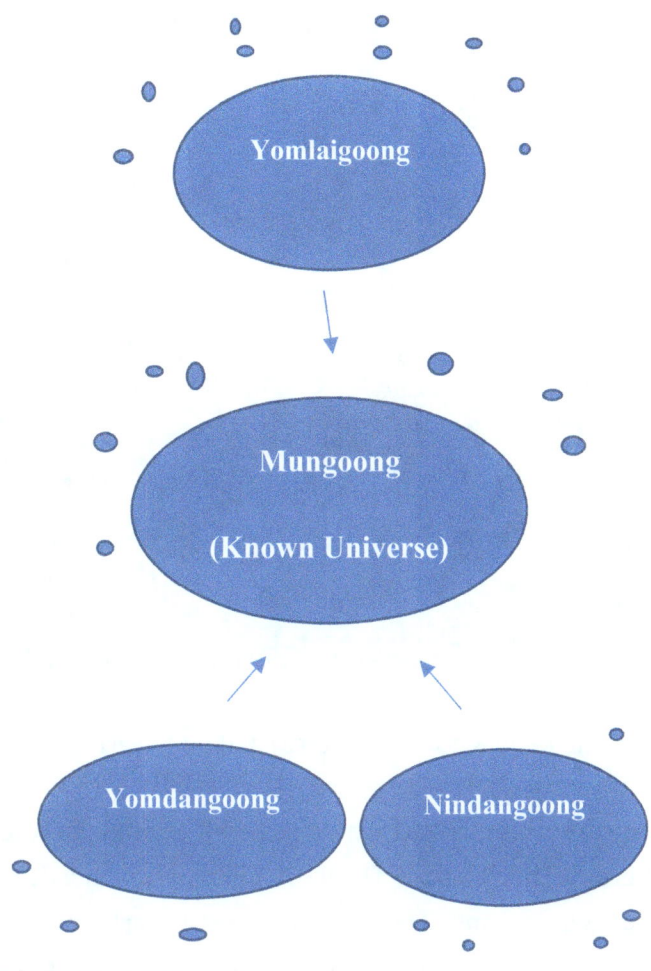

Mungoong (The Known Universe) was created about 300 trillion earth years ago by the merging of three prehistoric Universes and their Dwarf Universes together. Of these three prehistoric Universes, Yomlaigoong was created by the merging of two older prehistoric Universes septillion earth years ago.

193

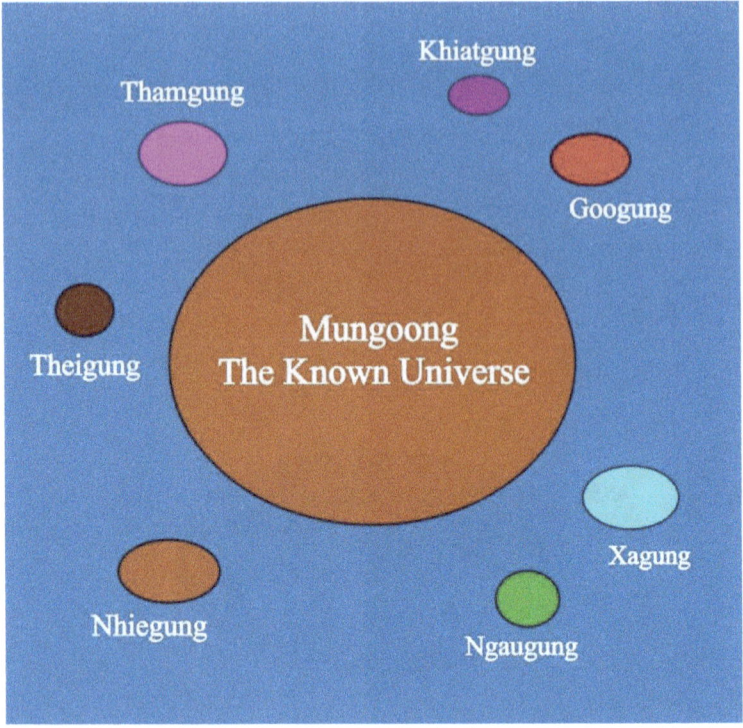

Mungoong (The Known Universe) and its Dwarf Universes.

There are seventh Dwarf Universes orbit around the Known Universe. The closest Dwarf Universe to the Known Universe is Xagung. The second closest Dwarf Universe to the Known Universe is Nhiegung. The third closest Dwarf Universe to the Known Universe is Thamgung. The fourth closest Dwarf Universe to the Known Universe Theigung. The fifth closest Dwarf Universe to the Known Universe Ngaugung. The sixth closest Dwarf Universe to the Known Universe Googung. The farthest Dwarf Universe to the Known Universe Khiatgung.

# Chapter 14

# The Merging

As the verses, galaxies, stars, and planets in the Goongverse are constantly evolving, changing and merging to serve the soul development purposes of all the entities in the Goongverse, the entities residing in the Goongverse are also evolving, changing and merging as they move from one dimension to another dimension and from one verse to another verse. As entities graduate from one dimension and move up to the next dimension in the Goongverse, many entities in the lower dimensions would merge together to become one entity in the higher dimensions. The entities that merge together to create one higher density entity in the same verse not necessarily have to come from the same planet; they can come from different planets within the same verse but make it to the graduation at the same spacetime. For example, when moving from the third dimension up to the fourth dimension, the graduate third density entities from Earth can merge with the graduate third density entities from other planets in the Known Universe who make it to the graduation at the same spacetime to form a fourth density entity when moving up to the fourth dimension.

When graduating from the second dimension and move up to the third dimension, about 100 second density entities who graduated from the second dimension would merge together to form the consciousness of one third density entity. When graduating from the third dimension and move up to the fourth dimension, about 100 third density entities who graduated from the third dimension would merge together to form the consciousness of one fourth density entity. When graduating from the fourth dimension and move up to the fifth dimension, about 100 fourth density entities who graduated from the fourth dimension would merge together to form the consciousness of one fifth density entity. When graduating from the fifth dimension and move up to the sixth dimension, about 100 fifth density entities who graduated from the fifth dimension would merge together to form the consciousness of one sixth density entity. When graduating from the sixth dimension and move up to the seventh dimension, about 100 sixth density entities who graduated from the sixth dimension would merge together to form the consciousness of one seventh density entity.

If put these numbers in the form of the third density entities to start with, it would take about 100 third density entities to form a fourth density entity, 10 thousand third density entities to form a fifth density entity, 1 million third density entities to form a sixth density entity, 100 million third density entities to form a seventh density entity, 10 billion third density entities to form an eighth density entity, and 1 quindecillion third density entities to form a twenty-seventh density entity. (Quindecillion is the measurement that has 48 zeros behind it).

The merging continues throughout the whole Goongverse. When the cosmic entities graduate and move from one verse to the next verse, they can merge with other entities from other verses who make it to the graduation at the same spacetime to become one entity in the higher verse in the goongversal hierarchy. For example, when moving from the Known Universe to the Multiverse where the Known Universe is located, the graduate seventh density entities in the Known Universe can merge with the other graduate seventh density entities from other Universes which also located within the same Multiverse to become one eight density entity in the Multiverse.

The merging of the goongversal entities stops at the twenty-seventh dimension. The twenty-seventh density entities when graduate from the Goongverse and move up to the Creatorverse, they no longer merge with any other twenty-seventh density entities who also graduate at the same spacetime to form one entity in the Creatorverse. They graduate and exit the Goongverse as each individual entity and move up to the Creatorverse to become the true cosmic creators. Once they move up to the Creatorverse, each of them can create his or her own verse in the Creatorverse before they start creating celestial objects, verses, or lifeforms in the Cosmos.

Many third density entities probably afraid that the merging of themselves with a few other third density entities to become one fourth density entity would make them loose their true selves. However, the merging doesn't make them loose a tiny bit of their true selves. They are still who they are, whatever personalities, consciousnesses, or experiences they have experienced, they all still present in the new fourth density entity. Not only they don't lose a tiny bit of their true selves, but they actually gain more knowledges, consciousnesses, and experiences through the merging. Suddenly they have access to all the knowledges, consciousnesses, and experiences of the other third density entities who just merged together with them. Anything that the other third density entities have experienced or been through, they would feel as if those were their own personal experiences. They would feel as if they have experienced all those experiences, knowledges, and consciousnesses by themselves personally. When a third density entity from Earth graduate and move up to the fourth dimension, he or she can merge with a few graduate third density entities from Earth and a few graduate third density entities from other planets in the Known Universe to form a fourth density entity. Whatever experiences the other third density entities have experienced from their home planets, the third density entity from Earth would feel as if those were his or her own experiences. He or she would feel as if he or she already lived through those experiences by herself or himself before personally.

When the goongversal entities from the twenty-seventh dimension exit the Goongverse and move up to the Creatorverse, they would remain as each individual entity. No merging occurs in the Creatorverse or the Godverse as well. If one day they no longer interested in being the cosmic creators in the Creatorverse or they no longer interested in creating celestial verses or celestial objects or celestial lifeforms, they can work their ways up to the Godverse. If they can raise up their vibrational frequencies to match with the vibrational frequencies of the Godverse, they then can move up to the Godverse to become the Deities or the Gods. They can stay in the Godverse to assist the Infinite Creator with the management of the Cosmos. When they have raised up their vibrational frequencies to match with the vibrational frequencies of the Infinite Godverse, they can move up to the Infinite Godverse and merge with the Infinite Creator to become one entity. Each time when there's a merge occurring in the Infinite Godverse, the power of the Infinite Creator would increase significantly. The process of moving up from the Creatorverse to the Godverse could take up hundred centillion earth years and the process of moving up from the Godverse to the Infinite Godverse could take up googolplex earth years.

The cosmic creators after graduating from the Goongverse and move up to the Creatorverse can choose to stay in the Creatorverse permanently as the Cosmic creators without moving up to the Godverse or the Infinite Godverse to merge with the Infinite Creator as one entity. It's a choice that they can make when they move up to the Creatorverse. Regardless of whatever they will choose, both paths are extremely adventurous and rewarding.

The Goongverse is like a tiny piece of sand in all the beaches in all the Universes, all the Multiverses, all the Megaverses, all the Gigaverses, all the Archverses, and the whole Goongverse combined in our Cosmos. There are so many voids and empty spaces in the Cosmos need to be filled with celestial objects and celestial lifeforms. The Infinite Creator is waiting in excitement for the future cosmic creators to finish their trainings in the Goongverse so they can move up to the Creatorverse where they would start creating celestial objects and celestial lifeforms which operate in brand-new cosmic structures and cosmic laws that he couldn't even think of creating.

Because the merging is happening in every dimension and every verse throughout the Goongverse, the third density entities on Earth should be aware that when they have the intention of trying to do something to harm others, they are actually harming their own selves. The third density entities from powerful countries which think they are better and more superior than the third density entities from other weaker countries before deciding to go to war or invade other countries, they should be aware that the people in the other countries that they are about to invade and kill are actually the entities who would merge with them to become one higher density entities in the distance future. They should know that killing the third density entities in other countries is actually killing their own selves or part of themselves. This kind of behavior will slow down the graduation process for both sides and it will hurt the soul development processes of both sides greatly. No entities would ever benefit from this type of childish behaviors. The entities who got killed would lose their chance to finish their third dimensional cosmic lessons in this incarnation in order to graduate, they then have to reincarnate back again to relearn their third dimensional cosmic lessons in their next incarnation. The entities that committed the killing can't be qualified for the graduation; therefore, they also have to reincarnate back again to relearn their third dimensional cosmic lessons in their next incarnation. When they reincarnate back as the third density entities on Earth in their next incarnation, they might get killed by the third density entities that they killed before in their previous incarnation. This process would repeat over and over again in many incarnations, which makes it impossible for the entities that got involved to make it to the graduation, therefore, it would slow down their graduation process greatly.

Earth is now in the graduation period. This is the graduation period of the third graduation cycle since the last genetic alteration. Any third density entities who have the desire to graduate in this graduation should really start focusing on their soul development processes and focusing on learning the third dimensional cosmic lessons. They have time from now until the year of 2071 to make it to the graduation in this third graduation cycle. If they can't make it to the graduation during this 50 earth years graduation period, they would have to wait for the next graduation cycle to take place which is another 75 thousand earth years. They would probably have to reincarnate hundred or thousand more times on Earth to learn the same third dimensional cosmic lessons over and over again until they finally learn their third dimensional cosmic lessons. Every time when they reincarnate back, they have to pass through the cosmic veil of forgetfulness and forget all about their previous life experiences, therefore, they would feel as if everything is fresh and brand-new to them. They would feel as if they have never been here on Earth before. They don't even realize that they probably have been on Earth for hundreds or thousands of times already.

All the third density entities on Earth should know that the time to make it to the graduation in this graduation cycle is now. Any later than that would be too late to make it to the graduation in this graduation cycle. It's time to wake up. It's time to focus on the soul development processes. It's time to learn the third dimensional cosmic lessons which are the lessons of love and compassion. It's time to end all wars, violences, and conflicts on Earth. It's time to stop sending troops across the borders. If any countries ever have the desire of sending something across the borders, send love, light, kindness, and help across the borders instead. It's time to know that all the third density entities on Earth are destined to become something much bigger and much greater, much more divine and much more powerful. All the third density entities were created for great purposes, not for coming here to the third dimension on Earth or on any other third dimensional planets in the universal verse to stay permanently without learning the third dimensional cosmic lessons which designed only for the cosmic preschoolers to learn. It's time for the third density entities on Earth and the third density entities on other third dimensional planets to graduate from the cosmic preschool and move up to the cosmic primary school. There are so many wonderful, unimaginable, and marvelous things for the third density entities to learn, to experience, and to explore as they move up higher and higher in the goongversal hierarchy. There are still so much of their cosmic power that hasn't been unlocked or activated yet. They still don't know what they are capable of building or creating. When they have learned all of their cosmic lessons in the lower dimensions and move up to the highest dimension in the goongversal hierarchy, they will be able to unlock all of their cosmic creator power. They will come to realize how powerful and how godly they really are. They all are the future cosmic creators.

It's time to wake up, the sleeping future cosmic creators!

It's time to realize that the existence of the third density entities in the Known Universe is only a brief moment in the grand timeline of the Goongverse. The existence of the goongversal entities is only a brief moment in the grand timeline of the Cosmos. The third density entities should do whatever they need to do here on Earth, learn whatever they need to learn here in the third dimension so they can move up to the higher dimensions where they can unlock more of their cosmic creator power. They can start building complex celestial objects and celestial lifeforms as they move up higher and higher in the goongversal hierarchy. Beyond the third dimension, entities from the higher dimensions already have the cosmic power to create planet and its moons, star systems, galaxies, dwarf galaxies, clusters of galaxies, Universes, clusters of universes, Multiverses, clusters of multiverses, Megaverses, clusters of megaverses, etc. Just imagine what they can build and create after they have finished all of their cosmic trainings in the twenty-seventh dimension in the creator school. They can build and create the unthinkable, the unimaginable, and the incomprehensible celestial objects or structures that are far more perfect and far more spectacular than the Goongverse itself.

It's time to wake up!

It's time to move up to the Creatorverse to help the Infinite Creator to build the most unique and the most marvelous Cosmos that has never been existed in the vast Grand Cosmos before. It's time to explore the other Cosmoses in the Grand Cosmos and to meet the Grand Infinite Creator of the Grand Cosmos with the Infinite Creator of our Cosmos.

# Chapter 15

# Summary and Final Thoughts

The Goongverse was created as a cosmic school for training and building future cosmic creators. It was created couple hundred decillion earth years ago by the Creator of the Goongverse. There are many verses in the Goongverse, the universal verse, the multiversal verse, the megaversal verse, the gigaversal verse, the archversal verse and the goongversal verse. There are many Universes in the universal verse, many Multiverses in the multiversal verse, many Megaverses in the megaversal verse, many Gigaverses in the gigaversal verse, and many Archverses in the archversal verse. There are twenty-seven dimensions in the Goongverse and each dimension offers unique and distinctive cosmic lessons for training the goongversal entities to become the future cosmic creators in the Creatorverse.

The Known Universe was created recently by the merging of the three prehistoric Universes and their Dwarf Universes. It was created more than 300 trillion earth years ago to serve the soul development purposes of the lower density entities in these three prehistoric Universes and their

Dwarf Universes who couldn't make it to the graduation and exit the universal verse. All lifeforms in the Known Universe originated from these three prehistoric Universes and their Dwarf Universes. The Milky Way galaxy is a newly form galaxy which located in the newly formed part of the Known Universe. Most of the stars and galaxies in the Observable Universe are also located in the newly formed part of the Known Universe. This is why scientists on Earth couldn't measure the exact age of the Known Universe. They can only measure the age of the newly formed celestial objects in the newly formed part of the Known Universe where the Earth is located.

In each individual Universe, when a planet no longer supporting the third dimensional lifeforms, the third dimensional lifeforms on that planet usually get transported to a younger planet which still supporting the third dimensional lifeforms and offering the third dimensional cosmic lessons. In the Known Universe, many planets currently no longer supporting the third dimensional lifeforms. Many of the third dimensional lifeforms on those planets got transported to Earth and to other third dimensional planets for them to relearn their third dimensional cosmic lessons. The third dimensional lifeforms on Earth originated from every part of the Known Universe. They aren't originated from Earth.

The third density entities on Earth originally had 13 strands of DNA and the capacity of their brains was 100%.

They were powerful cosmic entities. In order to keep them from being able to develop advanced technologies and powerful weapons that could end up leading themselves to destruction or extinction before they could learn their third dimensional cosmic lessons on Earth, the Universal Council and the Galactic Council in the Known Universe decided to alter some of their DNA to serve the purposes of their soul development. The Universal Council and the Galactic Council decided to reduce their DNA from 13 strands to 10 strands, then to 8 strands, then to 6 strands, then to 4 strands, and finally reduced to 2 strands. With only two strands of DNA left, the third density entities on Earth at this current spacetime are not as strong and as powerful as their ancestors in the past. However, they are possessing one of the most powerful cosmic protection charms in the Known Universe which is the human free will.

As the DNA of the third density entities on Earth got reduced, their lifespan also got reduced significantly. Therefore, the graduation cycle also got reduced from every 200 thousand earth years to every 75 thousand earth years. The duration of each graduation is about 50 earth years. Earth is currently in the graduation period of the third graduation cycle since the last genetic alteration. The duration of this graduation period will end in the year of 2071 on Earth. Whoever cannot make it to the graduation in this graduation cycle will have to wait another 75 thousand earth years for the next graduation cycle to take place.

There are many cosmic workers volunteering on Earth at this current spacetime to help with the graduation process.

Because of the negative energy constantly got infused into the Goongverse by the Anti Creator, any entities in any dimensions in the Goongverse can get affected and turn to polarize negatively. Negative polarized entities can only move from one dimension to the next dimension within the same verse. They cannot move from one verse to the next verse in the Goongversal hierarchy. When the negative polarized entities reach the highest sub-dimension of the dimension below the highest dimension in their host verse, the resetting process will take place. They will be reset to the dimensions where they first started to polarize negatively for them to relearn their cosmic lessons again.

Everything in the Goongverse is constantly evolving, changing, and merging. Many Archverses, Gigaverses, Megaverses, Multiverses, Universes, Galaxies, stars, planets, and living lifeforms have come and gone, have changed forms, and have merged together since the day the Goongverse was created. Many entities existed in the past no longer existing in the same forms as the past at this current spacetime. Many entities exist at this current spacetime won't be existing in the same forms as in the future because of the merging which constantly taking place in every verse and every dimension in the Goongverse.

The Goongverse was created for building future cosmic creators, in order for the future cosmic creators be able to graduate and exit the Goongverse, they must learn all the twenty-seventh dimensional cosmic soul lessons in the Goongverse and be able to balance out their soul development processes with their creator power. When their creator power surpasses their soul development processes, extinction usually occurs. It had happened many times in many dimensions and many verses in the Goongverse. It had happened to the Known Universe. It had happened to planets in the Solar System. It had happened to civilizations on Earth as well. Earth is in the duration of the third graduation cycle since the last genetic alteration. However, advanced technology developments have been accelerating at this current spacetime. The Universal Council and the Galactic Council are watching closely to see if majority of the third density entities on Earth would be able to make it to the graduation before they could develop some kind of advanced technologies or powerful weapons that might end up destroying themselves or leading themselves to destruction. Many higher density entities are watching this graduation cycle closely as well. Everyone is waiting to see how many third density entities on Earth could make it to the graduation in this graduation cycle. Earth has become very crowded because none of the third density entities got transported to Earth have made it to the graduation in the previous graduation cycles.

Despite the fact that the Universal Council and the Galactic Council already reduced the DNA of the third density entities on Earth from 13 strands to only 2 strands, some groups of the third density entities on Earth in the recent past still be able to develop advanced technologies and powerful weapons that ended up leading themselves to destruction. The testing of powerful weapons not only lead the Atlantis civilization to the path of extinction but it also caused the split between the South America Continent and the Africa Continent. It wasn't because of the earth plates were moving. For sure the earth plates are constantly moving and have caused many minor splits in Earth's history, but for the split between the South America Continent and the Africa Continent, it was the result of advanced and powerful weapon testing.

At this current spacetime, with the help of many negative polarized entities from the higher dimensions, the third density entities on Earth are in the path of developing advanced technologies and powerful weapons that are totally out of their control. With the development of artificial intelligence in recent spacetime, the third density entities on Earth are facing great threat. This advanced technology could end up wiping all the third density entities out before they could even make it to the graduation. The third density entities on Earth should be aware of the consequences of developing technologies that are totally out of their control. They should only try to develop something that still staying within their limit of control. If they develop something smarter than them and they have absolutely no control over it, the outcome would be devastating. The third density entities on Earth should look at the past, look at planet Kong, look at the Atlantis civilization, see how dangerous advanced technologies and powerful weapons can do to a planet and its civilizations. Do not try to put the third density entities on Earth in the path of extinction by focusing on developing advanced technologies that are totally out of human control. Try to balance out between the soul development processes and technology developments. Live in harmony with nature. Technologies to certain point can help make life easier and simpler for the third density entities on Earth. However, when technologies are too advanced and out of the third density entities control. Destruction and extinction always occur. This already happened in the Solar System's history and on Earth's history before. Planet Kong in the Solar System got blew up and turned into the Asteroid Belt between Mars and Jupiter. The Atlantis civilization on Earth developed advanced technologies and powerful weapons that ended up leading themselves to destruction. The third density entities on Earth should exercise their creator power carefully at this current spacetime. Beware that certain technologies could be given to them by the higher negative polarized density entities with the purpose of letting them using it to destroy their own civilizations. The third density entities on Earth should only develop technologies that are still staying within their limit of control.

Besides the danger of developing advanced technologies and weapons that are out of the third density entities control which could end up leading the third density entities on Earth to destruction or extinction, wars also pose threats and slow down the soul development processes of the third density entities on Earth greatly. It's understandable that there are so many differences between the third density entity groups on Earth since each group came from different part of the Known Universe. Many of these groups even came from the three prehistoric Universes and their Dwarf Universes after the merging occurred and have never been able to make their ways up beyond the third dimension. Despite the fact that there are so many differences between each individual group, all the third density entities on Earth should know that they all come from the same stardust in the Cosmos. The iron in their blood is the same iron that can be found in any star explosions. They all are the future cosmic creators. At certain dimensions above the third dimension, they might merge together to become one higher density entity. In order for the third density entities to move up to the higher dimensions, wars on Earth need to be stopped. Any entities on Earth at this current spacetime who are holding great power and have the intention of igniting wars with other countries should realize that going to war with other countries only slow down their own personal development processes. No benefit has ever come from such ignorant, foolish, and childish behaviors.

Nothing in the Goongverse is permanent. The existence of the third density entities on Earth or on any other third dimensional planets is only a brief moment in the grand timeline of the Cosmos. No entities should let this short brief moment of existence in the third dimension slow down their process of becoming greater entities in the higher dimensions. No entities should let this short brief moment of existence in the third dimension stops them from becoming the future cosmic creators which they are destined to become. They shouldn't do harm to anyone in their journeys of becoming the cosmic creators. If they do harm to others, they are harming their own selves by slowing down their own processes. This existence is not permanent; this incarnation is not permanent either. Any entities who are holding great power in this incarnation should use it to help other entities around them. This can help them earn their tickets to the graduation. If they can't make their ways to the graduation because they haven't done enough good deeds for others or haven't finished learning their third dimensional cosmic lessons, at least when they reincarnate back to Earth to relearn their third dimensional cosmic lessons again, they would benefit from the kindness that they have given out in this incarnation. The entities they help in this incarnation would definitely try to pay them back in their next incarnation. If the third density entities who are holding great power on Earth at this current spacetime use it for their own benefits or to harm other entities, in their next incarnation they would suffer greatly from it. The third density entities who are holding great power on Earth should know that they might be powerful in this incarnation, but in their next incarnation, there's no guarantee that they would hold the same power again. They are more likely to reincarnate in the position of the entities that they did harm to in their previous incarnation so that they can learn the lessons and understand the pain and suffering they had caused for others. The entities who are holding great power in this incarnation should try to use it for a good cause. Chances are they might be able to make it to the graduation in this graduation cycle because of the good deeds they have done. If they couldn't make it to the graduation in this graduation cycle, at least in their next incarnation, they would benefit greatly from the kindness they have given out in this incarnation. If an entity that they offered their kindness to in this incarnation be able to make his or her way to the graduation and move up to the fourth dimension, he or she definitely would try to come back to the third dimension to offer help to the entities who had helped him or her before in the third dimension.

The third density entities who are holding great power at this current spacetime on Earth should really exercise their power carefully so it would benefit them in their journeys of becoming the true cosmic creators. They shouldn't use it to harm others. Harming others is harming their own selves. The entities that do harm to others are the entities that usually suffer the consequences the most from their own actions. If they don't pay for the consequences in this incarnation, they would pay for the consequences in their next incarnation. It's the lesson that they need to learn in order for them to growth to become better cosmic entities.

The journey of becoming the cosmic creators can be fast or slow, pleasant or painful, it all depends on each individual's behaviors and the energy that they are sending out. The entities that do harm to others with the power they have only brings in pain, misery, and suffering into their journeys. They might be happy and powerful in one incarnation, but suffering so much in many incarnations after. Therefore, the third entities should exercise the power they have at hands carefully. They shouldn't invite any pain, misery, or suffering into their journeys. They should invite happiness, joy, bliss, pleasure, and merriness into their journeys instead.

The time for the graduation is here. All the future cosmic creators on Earth should look deep within them, find out who they really are and the reasons why they are here on Earth at this current spacetime. They should be able to realize that they are here to learn the third dimensional cosmic lessons, the lessons of love and compassion. They should start spending time learning their cosmic lessons so they can move up to the fourth dimension and higher. There are so many wonders and excitements waiting for them to explore in the fourth dimension and above. They shouldn't delay their own journey by trying to develop advanced technologies and weapons that could end up terminate their own selves before they could make it to the graduation and move up to the higher dimensions. They should know that every time when they fail to learn their cosmic lessons, they have to reincarnate back in the same dimension to relearn the same cosmic lessons again. If they keep repeating the same cosmic lessons over and over again in many incarnations, this would greatly slow down their journeys of becoming the future cosmic creators. Many of their third density cosmic fellows from the three prehistoric Universes had made their ways up to the twenty-seventh dimension and ready to exit the Goongverse to become the true cosmic creators in the Creatorverse while they are still here in the third dimension trying to learn their third dimensional cosmic lessons over and over again. Their cosmic fellows in the twenty-seventh dimension are surprised to see some of the third density entities from the three prehistoric Universes are still here in the third dimension trying to learn their third dimensional cosmic lessons. They have sent out services to help the third density entities from the twenty-seventh dimension, but the third density entities on Earth and on other third dimensional planets in the Known Universe couldn't receive it because of their low vibrational frequencies in the third dimension.

It's time for the third density entities on Earth to wake up. It's time for them to finish learning their third dimensional cosmic lessons so they can graduate and move up to the fourth dimension or higher. There are so many wonderful and marvelous things in the higher dimensions that are waiting for them to discover and explore. There's so much cosmic creator power within them that hasn't been unlocked.

Just imagine what they can create when they unlock more and more of the cosmic creator power within them when they move up to the higher dimensions. Just imagine what they can create when they are in the fourth, the fifth, the sixth or the seventh dimensions. They can create a planet and its moons when they are in the fourth dimension. They can create a star system like the Solar System when they are in the fifth dimension. They can create a galaxy like the Milky Way galaxy when they are in the sixth dimension. They can create a cluster of galaxies like the Virgo cluster or supercluster of galaxies like the BOSS Great Wall when they are in the seventh dimension. As they graduate from the Known Universe and move up to the Multiverse where the Known Universe is located, they can create a Universe like the Known Universe they are currently residing in. Just imagine what they can create as they unlock their creator power when they move up higher and higher in the goongversal hierarchy. They would be able to create the unimaginable, the unthinkable, and the impossible celestial objects that they would never have thought of with their 3D functional brains. It's time to wake up. It's time to learn their third dimensional cosmic lessons. It's time to move up to the fourth dimension and higher. It's time to unlock more of the cosmic creator power within them. It's time to do the impossible that they have never thought of doing before.

Wake up, the future cosmic creators!

# About the Author

Triple T is a third density entity on Earth like any of you at this current spacetime in this third dimension. The only difference is that she had been programmed with a teeny tiny bit of the cosmic knowledge to deliver. Many cosmic workers from the higher dimensions in the Known Universe also have been programmed with the universal knowledge of the Known Universe to deliver to the third density entities on Earth. Triple T doesn't have any desires to seek for fame or popularity in this brief third dimensional existence on Earth in the grand timeline of the Cosmos, therefore, she would like to keep her third dimensional identity anonymous. Whatever needed to be shared for the purpose of serving her cosmic mission here on Earth, she already shared in this book. For we all are powerful cosmic entities here on Earth to learn our cosmic lessons as the preschoolers or here on Earth to assist other preschoolers to learn their cosmic lessons, fame and popularity in this short existence of the third dimension doesn't matter a bit in the grand time line of the Goongverse or in the grand timeline of the Cosmos.

Triple T doesn't take any credits for her work in this book since everything comes from the divine realm. She's only here to serve the cosmic mission she had signed up for like any other cosmic workers. She's grateful to be here in the third dimension at this current spacetime to offer a little help to all of you, the powerful future cosmic creators, when you are still in your primitive form in the third dimension.

Triple T would like to dedicate this book to all the higher density entities from the divine realm and all the higher density entities from the Known Universe who are currently volunteering here on Earth. Without the guidance and help from the higher density entities, she wouldn't be able to wake up to carry out her mission here on Earth in this incarnation. She's really grateful to all the higher density entities who have been very patient with her and have never given up on her during her long awakening process on Earth.

Triple T is also very grateful to have a chance to meet many of you, the future cosmic creators, in your primitive form on Earth before you make your ways up to the Creatorverse to become the true cosmic creators. She's grateful to each and every entity she has met here on Earth. She's grateful to each and every entity who have been reading this book. Hopefully with a teeny tiny bit of the cosmic knowledge she provided in this book, many of you would be able to make your ways up to the Creatorverse faster than you have ever expected or imagined. Many of you probably don't believe a thing mentioning in this book and probably think that this book is talking about nonsense stuffs. It's understandable since no one can force the truth, wisdom, or knowledge on anyone else. Everyone must experience it, feel it, see it, touch it, and understand it by themselves in order to believe in it. The best way for you to find out the truth and the purpose of your existence here on Earth or in the Goongverse is to learn your third dimensional cosmic lessons and move up to the higher dimensions in the goongversal hierarchy to find out the truth by yourself.


See you all in the Creatorverse!

Triple T

# Table of Large Numbers

| Number of 0 | Name | Abbreviation |
|:---:|:---:|:---:|
| 3 | Thousand | K |
| 6 | Million | M |
| 9 | Billion | B |
| 12 | Trillion | T |
| 15 | Quadrillion | Q |
| 18 | Quintillion | QN |
| 21 | Sextillion | S |
| 24 | Septillion | SP |
| 27 | Octillion | O |
| 30 | Nonillion | N |
| 33 | Decillion | D |
| 36 | Undecillion | U |
| 39 | Duodecillion | DD |
| 42 | Tredecillion | TD |
| 45 | Quattuordecillion | QD |
| 48 | Quindecillion | QND |
| 51 | Sexdecillion | SD |
| 54 | Septendecillion | SPD |
| 57 | Octodecillion | OD |
| 60 | Novemdecillion | ND |
| 63 | Vigintillion | VT |
| 66 | Unvigintillion | UVT |
| 69 | Duovigintillion | DVT |

| | | |
|---|---|---|
| 72 | Trevigintillion | TVT |
| 75 | Quattuorvigintillion | QVT |
| 78 | Quinvigintillion | QNVT |
| 81 | Sexvigintillion | SVT |
| 84 | Septenvigintillion | SPVT |
| 100 | Googol | |
| 303 | Centillion | |
| 100<br>10<br>10 | Googolplex | |
| | | |

# Notes from Triple T to the Third Density Entities that Are Worth Reading

In your journey of becoming the future cosmic creator, sometimes your patience can be tested. Just because something doesn't happen exactly like the way you wanted it to happen, it doesn't mean that it won't happen. You just have to wait patiently and remain positive. Remaining positive is the best way to stop any negative energy or any negative entities from interfering with your manifestation process. Eventually when no negative energy or no negative entity interfering with the process, whatever you want to happen, it will happen. This is one of the secrets to successfully manifest anything you want in life in this third dimension or any other dimensions in the Goongverse.

Your thoughts and your imaginations are far more powerful than you could even realize. You can manifest anything in this third dimension or in any other dimensions in the Goongverse using your thoughts and your imaginations. Don't forget that the whole Goongverse was created by the Thought entity after all.

You can manifest anything you want in any dimensions as long as your manifestation doesn't hurt or harm any other entities on purpose. When your manifestation hurts or harms any other entities on purpose, you must pay for the consequences sooner or later. There's no way around it. It's part of the cosmic lessons every entity must learn in order to graduate to become the cosmic creators in the Creatorverse.

Never ever try to harm any entities on purpose or giving a hard time to any entities with the power you have at hand. You are open up the door to invite pain and misery into your journey. For whatever you put the other entities through, you must go through it except it could be 100 times harder so you can learn your cosmic lesson of being kind. Use the power you have at hand to do good for others. Once you start doing good for others, you will see miracles happening to you every day.

Be kind to everyone. Be kind to the most unkind entities because kindness is what they needed the most. Kindness can help change and transform them to become kinder and better entities. Kindness and love have the power of transforming a negative polarized entity into a positive polarized entity.

At certain time in your journey in the Goongverse from the fourth dimension and up, you can choose to learn your cosmic lessons as a planetary entity if you choose to. You're allowed to learn the cosmic lessons as a planetary entity at least once. If you choose to learn it in any dimensions from the fourth dimension up to the seventh dimension in the universal verse, you don't have the choice of learning your lesson as a planetary entity in any verses after in the goongversal hierarchy. You can make that choice anytime when you move through the graduation portals. It means that you can become a star or a planet in the Known Universe one day if you choose to learn your higher dimensional cosmic lessons as a planetary entity in the universal verse. Choosing to learn your cosmic lessons as a planetary entity requires a lot of patience and tolerance. You must learn to be patient and tolerant with all the entities you're harboring. If you don't have enough patience and tolerance, you might terminate the learning process of many entities you're harboring when you express a bit of your frustration or anger. A bit of your frustration or anger can cause great damage to the lives of many entities you're harboring. These entities would have to reincarnate back again to continue learning their cosmic lessons since you terminate their learning process in this incarnation due to the way you express your frustration or anger. To make it easier to understand, just imagine if planet Earth expresses a bit of her frustration or anger, it would come in the form of natural disasters, many third density entities on Earth would lose their lives due to the natural disasters, therefore, their learning process would be terminated in that incarnation, they would have to reincarnate back again to continue learning their cosmic lessons in their next incarnation. Learning cosmic lessons as planetary entities is for building patience, tolerance, and nurturing into the future cosmic creators.

As you are learning your cosmic lessons, planet Earth is also learning her cosmic lessons as well.

Planetary entities (planets and stars) also go through the graduation process by merging with other planetary entities to become higher density entities to continue learning their next level of cosmic lessons and to support the higher density entities learning their cosmic lessons.

The Kuiper Belt used to be a planet before it got blew up into pieces because of the conflict between the fourth negative polarized density entities and the fourth positive polarized density entities when they first got transported to the Solar System to continue learning their fourth dimensional cosmic lessons from other older star systems in the Known Universe. The Kuiper Belt was known as planet Ji-X to the intelligent lifeforms in the Solar System. Some fourth density entities still residing in the Kuiper Belt at this current space time. However, they are not actively participating in the activities of the Solar System. They are currently still in the healing process after the destruction they have caused to planet Ji-X when they first got transported to the Solar System.

Not every entity after leaving their third physical bodies on Earth would move up to the lower astral plane in between the third and the fourth dimension to wait for their next incarnation. Some entities couldn't detach themselves from the experiences they had here on Earth in their most recent incarnation. Therefore, they keep staying behind on Earth and wandering around trying to interfere with the daily life of the third density entities. Some of these entities might have been wandering around for thousands of earth years. The third density entities referring to these entities as ghosts. If any entities on Earth have the ability to see these wandering entities, please kindly pray for them or talk to them to make them understand that they should leave everything behind on Earth in this incarnation and go to the lower astral plane between the third and the fourth dimension so they can reincarnate back to Earth to continue learning their cosmic lessons in their next incarnation. This will help them stop wasting their time wandering on Earth and help them speed up their learning process. Be the lighting candle for these wandering entities whenever you can. Many cosmic workers come to Earth with the mission of being the lighting candles to guide these wandering entities so they don't get lost in their journeys of becoming the future cosmic creators.

Every cosmic volunteer worker on Earth or on any other third dimensional planets in the Known Universe has a cosmic ID. If you happen to remember your cosmic ID or found out your cosmic ID through your dreams, never ever give it out to any entities, especially those entities that trying to approach you in your dreams to ask for your name, your date of birth, or your cosmic ID. Those are the negative polarized entities from the higher dimensions who are trying to terminate your volunteer mission here on Earth. Try not to give out your name, your date of birth, or your cosmic ID to any entities you meet in your dreams. If the entities you meet in your dreams are your higher self or your spiritual guides or the entities from the Galactic Council, they already know exactly who you are, they don't need to ask you for your name, your date of birth, or your cosmic ID. The negative polarized entities from the higher dimensions don't know exactly who you are even though they have the ability to detect the divine light that you emitting out and your high vibrational frequencies. They know that you're a cosmic worker from the higher dimension, but they don't know your exact identity. As long as they don't know your exact identity like your name, your date of birth or your cosmic ID, they can't do anything to harm you telepathically. Negative polarized density entities from the higher dimensions tend to approach the cosmic workers through their dreams to ask for their identities so they can use it to harm the cosmic workers telepathically and use it to terminate their volunteer missions here on Earth.

The best way to travel in the Known Universe or in any other Universes is not through spaceships at the speed of light or through space portals. Traveling through spaceships at the speed of light or through space portals is only for the third density entities who haven't been awakened and are not ready to graduate to move up to the fourth dimension yet. From the fourth dimension up to the seventh dimension in the universal verse, entities can travel easily within their host Universe in couple of milliseconds. Entities beyond the universal verse can travel within their host verse in a blink of an eye. For the cosmic workers volunteering on the third dimensional planets who are already awakened and the third density entities who are ready to graduate and move up to the fourth dimension, they can travel anywhere within their host Universe when they temporary detach their true selves out of their third dimensional physical bodies. Their third dimensional physical bodies are not capable of traveling telepathically. They must travel through spaceships at the speed of light or through space portals. From the fourth dimension and up, entities can travel through space with their astral bodies, therefore, they don't have to detach themselves out of their astral bodies whenever they traveling through space. The third density entities on Earth at this current spacetime still dreaming of building spaceships that can travel at the speed of light so they can travel to the nearby planets while they don't know that many cosmic workers on Earth who are already awakened and the third density entities on Earth who are ready to graduate and move up to the fourth dimension already be able to travel back and forth between planets, star systems, and galaxies in the Known Universe within couple of milliseconds. Since higher density entities can travel through space with their astral bodies, they can appear and disappear seemingly out of nowhere. Scientists on Earth have been puzzling with this cosmic phenomenon since the day quantum computer has been developed. They still don't quite understand why particle in space can appear and disappear seemingly out of nowhere. This is simply because as more and more cosmic power being unlocked in the higher dimensions, higher density entities are capable of doing things that are far more beyond the comprehension and the imagination of any third density entities on Earth.

What's consider as dark matter to scientists on Earth are simply particle and higher density entities from the higher dimensions in the Known Universe that technologies on Earth not yet capable of detecting or observing. Scientists on Earth so far only capable of detecting the gravitational effects of these entities on visible matter such as galaxies or galaxy clusters but not capable of detecting or observing their activities yet. Dark matter or higher density entities do emit, absorb, and reflect light, but the type of light that technologies on Earth not yet capable of detecting at this current spacetime.

Nothing exist randomly in the Goongverse, everything is created to serve the purposes of training the future cosmic creators. Whatever theories that scientists on Earth have regarding to the origins or the formations of the Known Universe up until this current spacetime are only the theories that trying to explain the formations of the newly formed celestial objects in the newly formed part of the Known Universe where the Earth is located, not the formation of the Known Universe itself or the formation of the whole Goongverse itself. Technologies and scientific knowledges on Earth or on any other third dimensional planets are far lack behind and not capable of explaining the origin or the formation of the Known Universe itself.

In your journey of becoming the true cosmic creator, no matter what you do or who you meet, try to infuse your love, kindness, and positivity into everything that you do and everyone that you meet, in no time, you will find yourself in the Creatorverse as a true cosmic creator who are ready to build and create the unthinkable celestial objects, verses, and celestial lifeforms that are far more beyond the imagination of any third density entities on Earth or any entities in the Goongverse.

In your journey of becoming the true cosmic creator, nothing would be too hard or too difficult for you once you come to know the purpose of your true existence in the Cosmos. You are capable of doing the unthinkable and the impossible. You are capable of doing the unimaginable. Never ever forget that you all are the powerful future cosmic creators after all.

It's time for you to do the unthinkable and the impossible that you have never thought of doing before!

Can't wait to see you all in the Creatorverse!

If you cannot relate or resonate to any experiences or any cosmic events mentioning in this book, don't let this book bother you. As already mentioned earlier, this book is a science fiction book since it mentions about cosmic events and cosmic phenomena that cannot be proven by any scientific knowledges or any technologies on Earth at this current space time.

For permission to use the copyright content in this book, please contact representative of Triple T through email: representative.triple.t@gmail.com